Praise for Kate Perry's Novels

"Perry's storytelling skills just keep getting better and better!"

—*Romantic Times Book Reviews*

"Can't wait for the next in this series...simply great reading. Another winner by this amazing author."

—*Romance Reviews Magazine*

"Exciting and simply terrific."

—*Romancereviews.com*

"Kate Perry is on my auto buy list."

—*Night Owl Romance*

"A winning and entertaining combination of humor and pathos."

—*Booklist*

Other Titles by Kate Perry

The Laurel Heights Series:

Perfect for You

Close to You

Return to You

Looking for You

Dream of You

Sweet on You

Tamed by You

Here with You

All for You

Mad About You

The Family and Love Series:

Project Date

Playing Doctor

Playing for Keeps

Project Daddy

The Guardians of Destiny Series:

Marked by Passion

Chosen by Desire

Tempted by Fate

Mad About You

Kate Perry

Phoenix Rising Enterprise, Inc.

Mad About You

Chapter One

GROUNDS FOR THOUGHT, the neighborhood café, had been transformed into a sultan's palace for Nicole's lingerie debut. Gauzy material hanging all over, seductive music, dim lighting...

For everyone else, there was romance and excitement in the air tonight. For Julie, it was hell. The lingerie show was about to start, and her freakin' orchid wouldn't drape properly.

Julie glared at it, knowing her frustration had nothing to do with the flower and everything to do with her nemesis and their impending duel. But all thoughts of flowers and evil florists vacated her mind when *he* caught her eye.

He was medium height, muscular without being bulky. She liked the way he was dressed: nice slacks and a T-shirt under a dressy jacket. She could tell they were good quality but unpretentious and comfortable looking. He had short hair, a strong chin, and a hint of stubble. He walked like he owned the world, confident and sure.

Kind of attractive.

Okay — really hot.

And he headed straight for her.

He stopped in front of her, so close she could see the dark flecks in his hazel eyes. "What's your name?" he asked.

His voice gave her goose bumps. She swallowed thickly. "Julie Miller."

"Julie Miller" — he stepped closer — "I'm going to kiss you."

She looked at his mouth. It was a nice mouth, not too thin, not too full. It looked like it might know what to do, but she figured she should check. "Are you a good kisser?"

"You tell me." He cupped the side of her face and lowered his lips to hers.

It started soft, as if he was giving her time to adjust to the feel of him. Even though he wasn't aggressive, he was still in charge.

She liked that. She'd gone out with way too many guys who were wimps. She appreciated the strength because, really, if a man were going to stay with her, he'd have to be strong to withstand her.

Was he?

She closed the remaining gap between them, wrapped her arms around his neck, and tested him with a real kiss.

He didn't miss a beat. His fingers tangled in her ponytail, holding her firm. He slanted his mouth and *took* her—lips, a little tongue, and a lot of heat.

A shiver of pleasure ran up her spine, and she hummed as she tried to get closer.

Somewhere, music began to play. She could feel her heart beating in time with the bass. She distantly realized that the lingerie show had started, but she really didn't care.

Reluctantly he lifted his head, his gaze searching hers. "I need to pay attention to the show."

She nodded, more interested in the huskiness of his voice and the evidence of his arousal pressed against her thigh than any lingerie. "Okay."

The corner of his mouth hitched. "Do you want to know my name?"

"Are we going to see each other again?"

"Yes," he said firmly. His hand still in her hair, he rubbed the corner of her mouth. "Scott Wright."

"Nice to meet you, Scott." She studied him. "Are you a serial killer?"

A glimmer of humor lit his eyes. "No."

"A polygamist?"

"Do I look like I have multiple wives?"

"No, but you also don't look like you'd walk up to a random stranger and kiss the bejesus out of her."

"I've never done that, and you're not random." He caressed the side of her face, as if memorizing her face. Then he lowered his lips to hers again.

Just like the first time, the kiss curled her toes. It fizzed all the way down her spine, out her limbs, and back. She'd never been kissed like this — wholehearted and without reservation. Unapologetically. Confidently.

She heard clapping. For a second she thought it was for them, but then she remembered what was going on. "We're in the middle of a lingerie show," she said against his lips.

"It's fitting since I want to take yours off."

She felt a tremor of excitement deep in her belly. Sign her up for *that*. "Probably not best to do it in front of all these people."

"Probably not." Putting space between them,

he ran a hand down her back. "Think there's a private space in the back?"

"They're using it as a dressing room."

"Damn."

He sounded so regretful that she had to kiss him again. She poured a whole lot of desire into it. It surprised her how much there was because she had too much on her plate to date to deal with a man. The San Francisco Flower Competition was weeks away and she was going to win this year.

Plus, she didn't know this man. At least she knew his name now.

Scott growled and caught her up closer. "We're going to do this again, but somewhere private."

"Okay."

"Soon."

She mentally ran through her workload. "How's Monday?"

"Too far away."

"It's Friday today."

"Like I said, too far away." He stroked her hair. "But I'll take what you give me. Do you have a card?"

With a little regret, she untangled herself from him and reached into her pocket. She always kept a few cards on her, the half-sized ones because women's jean pockets were never functional.

He studied it and then slipped it into his inside coat pocket. "I'll call you."

"Okay."

"See you Monday, Julie." He kissed her again, slow and lingering, before he went to watch the show.

Maybe he'd come see her again after it was over. She could hope. She watched him take in the lingerie show. He watched with an intensity that had nothing to do with the scantily clad women. It almost seemed like he was more interested in how other people were reacting to Nicole's lingerie line.

The show ended to explosive applause, but she missed it all. She couldn't look away from Scott. She saw him go over to Nicole, hug her, and whisper something in her ear. Nicole clenched him tight, and then laughed happily as she let him go.

Did they know each other? Julie knew Nicole was in a relationship with Griffin Chase, the rock star. It was how she'd met the designer in the first place — he'd hired Julie to deliver flowers to Nicole every other day.

Crazy man. But he was a celebrity, and in her experience, all celebrities were wacky.

Scott said something more to Nicole and then left the café. Julie stared after him, disappointed that he didn't come back to her. Which also crazy, because she hadn't known him half an hour ago.

"I saw you making out in the corner," a sultry feminine voice said.

Talk about wacky celebrities... Julie didn't have to look to know who it was. "Bite me."

"It looks like he beat me to it." Sophie Martineau laughed, low and husky, as she slipped her arm around Julie's waist. "So?"

She knew what the actress was fishing for. She also knew she'd give in and tell her, but she didn't have to make it easy. "So, what?"

"I've known you an eon — "

"A year and a half," Julie corrected.

"Exactly, and in that time you've never been impulsive about anything, much less a man."

Yeah, it was baffling. "I'm going through a phase."

Sophie's lips pursed in her world-famous pout. "Are you really going to hold out on your BFF?"

Somehow, impossibly, Hollywood's hottest siren really *was* her BFF. As if life wasn't quirky enough. "He asked me out."

"Looks like he also checked your tonsils."

Sophie poked her. "Well? When are you going out with him?"

"You think I said yes?"

"Honey, you practically invited him to take your clothes off in front of all these people."

Julie blushed. That was a little too close to the truth. "It'd be stupid to go out with him right now. I need to focus on my entry for the San Francisco Flower Competition if I'm going to win."

"Forget the flower competition," Sophie said.

"I can't." She'd lost five years running, each year to Dr. Hyacinth Gardner, poseur of the floral universe. This year she was going to kick Hyacinth's ass and take home the trophy.

Sophie shook her head. "I didn't ask you if you were stupid. I asked when you were going out with him."

"Monday," she mumbled.

"Then I'll see you Sunday."

"Why?"

"So I can make sure you dress properly for your date."

She frowned down at her clothes. "What's wrong with what I'm wearing?"

Sophie lifted her brow. "Do you really want me to answer that?"

She and her friend were on opposite ends of the spectrum. Sophie always left home immaculately dressed but she had paparazzi following her all the time. Flowers didn't care if Julie ponytailed her hair and wore jeans every day. "Don't you have something better to do? Like torturing some poor Hollywood director or something?"

"Why, when I can torture you?" Sophie squeezed her shoulders. "See you Sunday. Try to remember to wash the dirt from your fingernails."

Frowning, Julie lifted her hands to inspect them. "I don't—"

Sophie chuckled as she sashayed back into the crowd.

"Damn it." She couldn't believe she fell for that. She glared at the woman as she slinked away. It was too bad she loved the actress, because it'd have been really satisfying to throw a vase of flowers at her head.

Chapter Two

KELLY "BULL" TORRES stood at the edge of the café, arms crossed, head bopping to the music as he watched the women parade down the runway in Nicole's creations. Grounds for Thought had pretty much been turned into a bordello for the lingerie show.

He'd met Nicole at his buddy Ethan's wedding and taken an instant liking to her. She was cute, like a kid sister. Even though he had nothing to do with her lingerie line, he felt pride as the first model paraded the fancy underwear she'd designed. He admired entrepreneurial moxie, and Nicole had it in spades.

He did, too. He knew when people looked at

him, they just saw a big bruiser who made a living beating other men to a pulp, but he'd been brought up in an entrepreneurial family. His grandfather had owned a number of successful bars, his dad started an automotive repair chain, and his brother was the taco truck king of the greater Northwest.

Now it was his turn.

The antsy feeling he'd carried with him lately flared, and he ruthlessly shut it down. He didn't need to stress about things; everything would work out. He'd found a group to back his smoothie business, and they were taking it national. It was just a matter of nailing down the details and signing the paperwork. Any day now. He needed to be patient.

He hated being patient. Waiting was not in his skill set. He always knew what he wanted, and he wanted it *now*.

He was on the cusp. He'd begun transitioning

out of mixed martial arts, and his smoothie line would be launched soon. He thought about the corset tucked away in the top drawer of his dresser. That red lace and silk was symbolic of this new chapter in his life, as well as a reminder that there was still one integral piece missing.

A woman.

Not just any woman. He wanted the one who'd fit the red corset he'd bought from Nicole last year.

That corset represented everything he wanted in a woman. Size-wise, yes. He liked his women bountiful. He was a big man and liked having something to hold on to. He always felt like he had to be careful with skinny women. He wanted a *woman* — someone who could hold her own with him.

More than that, though, he wanted someone who'd pull off wearing the corset with aplomb. A smart, bold, sexy woman who knew how to bring her man to his knees. *That* was who he wanted.

Like the goddess who stepped onto the makeshift runway and began strutting her stuff through the room.

"Hello," he said under his breath, coming to attention. She walked like she owned the world, her round hips swaying with sassy attitude.

He loved that. And, hot damn, she was gorgeous. Sultry eyes and a mouth that begged to be loved. Her bouncy hair was long and trailed over her creamy shoulders. And her curves...

Delicious.

Quietly, still watching her, Bull snuck up next to Nicole and whispered, "Who's that?"

"Joey?" Nicole asked, nodding at his goddess. "She lives in the neighborhood. She shops at Romantic Notions."

He growled low and deep in his throat. "She looks like my size."

"She is, actually."

"I could tell."

Smiling, Nicole patted his arm. "She'll be around after the show."

"I'm gonna make sure of it." He kissed her cheek and went to wait for his moment.

When the last model strode out wearing white bridal lingerie, the entire room burst into applause.

This was his chance. He wove his way through the crowd to the spot where he'd seen her hanging out with the other models.

When he got there she was gone.

He looked around the café but didn't spot her, but he noted a couple of the other women disappearing into the back area. She'd gone to change, most likely. He wasn't about to lose the chance to ask her out, so he lounged against the wall in the back, waiting.

He *really* hated waiting.

He smiled at the woman who emerged from the back, trying to look innocuous, which was pretty much impossible for someone like him.

Finally, she came out, dressed like a librarian, in a skirt that hit her knees and a little jacket. Her hair was pulled back in one of those fancy twists women magically knew how to do. Even buttoned up the way she was, she was sexy, and he wanted her.

He pushed away from the wall.

Her beautiful eyes met his.

His heart seized. He touched his chest, hoping he wouldn't keel over before he got one taste of her luscious lips.

Taking a deep breath, he cleared his throat, catching himself before saying *I have a corset in my closet I'd like you to try on*. Even he knew that was creepy. It was a conversation for the next time. For now, he dazzled her with a wholehearted, "Hi."

He mentally smacked his own head. *Hi?* That was the best he could do when he faced the woman of his dreams?

Joey smiled at him and said in a Southern accent, "Hello."

Her honey voice melted him, but her polite smile made him want to grab her by the hair and kiss genuine emotion into her expression.

Somehow he managed to restrain himself. He stuck out his hand. "I'm Bull."

She reluctantly shook his hand but let it go very quickly. "Nice to meet you," she said, her tone insincere.

Leaning, he lowered his voice said, "This is where you tell me your name."

"Joey," she replied after a pause.

So she was going to be difficult, huh? Game on. "Your mom named you Joey?"

The fine skin of her forehead furrowed. "No, she named me Josephine Belle."

"Josephine Belle," he drawled, testing it on his tongue. It was mysterious and full of curves. Round on his tongue. Perfectly *her*. He hummed appreciatively.

Her eyes widened, and she took the smallest

step back. "No one calls me that anymore, not since my mama died."

"Even better." He stepped forward. "What do you do for a living, Josephine Belle?"

"Why?"

"Because I want to know whether you're free to go out during the day or at night."

"Neither," she said firmly.

"You work all the time?"

"No." Her adorable nose wrinkled. "You're free to go out at any time?"

"My schedule is flexible." It was a vague answer, but he didn't want to get into his recent career quandary.

"Are you a consultant?" She looked him up and down like she couldn't picture it.

Smart woman. He'd go postal if he had to sit at a desk all day. "I dabble. So tell me when you'll go out with me."

A wall in the form of a polite smile went up.

"It's sweet of you to ask," she said in her steamy Southern voice, "but I'm not available."

Was she taken? He lifted her left hand and looked at her ring finger. No ring, no tan line. Keeping her hand, he scowled at her. "You dating someone?"

"Well, no." Blinking like it was a foreign concept, she retracted her hand.

He felt the slow slide of her palm against his like an intimate caress. He resisted the urge to throw her over his shoulder and carry her away. He doubted she'd appreciate that much enthusiasm so soon.

Instead he calmly said, "Then we can go to dinner. There's a great French bistro in the Marina that serves the best pork chops—"

"No, thank you."

Again with that polite, vague smile. He'd kiss it off her mouth if he didn't think she'd smack him upside the head.

She must have sensed the direction his thoughts had taken, because her eyes widened and she stepped aside. "I need to go mingle. Excuse me."

"I—"

"It was nice meeting you," she lied as she quickly rejoined the party.

He watched her disappear into the crowd. He could follow her, but he knew she'd make a quick getaway.

He stuck his hands in his pockets. Well, that wasn't exactly the way he wanted to start off with the woman he was going to spend the rest of his life with.

Chapter Three

His GRANDFATHER HAD always told him he'd know The One when he kissed her.

His grandfather was right.

Scott leaned back in his chair, propping his feet on the desk. He'd left the lights dimmed, sitting in the soothing shadows of his home office.

Only he wasn't soothed, not with the lingering taste of Julie Miller's kiss on his lips. He reached for his glass, the whiskey purely medicinal tonight, to calm himself. But no amount of whiskey was going to cure what ailed him: waiting till Monday to see Julie didn't make him happy.

He wasn't the sort of man who waited. Patience

wasn't one of his virtues: he identified what he wanted and then went for it.

He *definitely* wanted Julie.

Grandpa Davis would have nodded and said, "Whatchya waiting for then, boy?"

Scott grinned, holding up his glass high to the portrait across the room. "Here's to you, Grandpa."

He and his sister Alexis had their mother's father to thank for being grounded. The Carrington-Wrights were an old San Francisco family, from back in the Gold Rush era. In the city, they were royalty, and when his mother had married into the family, she'd embraced all the excess that came with the name and money.

It would have been easy for his sister and him to grow up to be like the entitled and spoiled people they'd gone to school with, but Grandpa Davis always said the family money wasn't their identity. It was a fail-safe and not something to rely on. The mark you made on the world was the measure of the person you were.

Somehow, he and his sister had managed to keep true to that. Scott had his venture capital company, and Alexis her fitness videos, which he'd helped launch. Scott went a step further, shortening his name to avoid riding on its prominence. He didn't want to live as Prescott Carrington-Wright III. Prescott Carrington-Wright III sounded like a pompous ass.

Grandpa Davis had taught them integrity, and loyalty, and the value of love. "Love trumps all, Scotty-boy," he used to say.

Scott sipped his whiskey, remembering how his grandfather used to sip whiskey as he told stories about him and Grandma Louise. How Davis had walked up to Louise and kissed her the first time he'd set eyes on her. How he'd always held her hand, right up to the very end when she'd passed away.

Scott wanted to be with someone whose hand he could hold, who'd hold his hand just as faithfully. Who saw him for who he was, and not what he was on paper.

Julie was it.

He used to question Davis about how he'd know. His grandpa had smiled and said he just would.

Grandpa Davis was right. The same way he knew when a company was a good investment, his gut told him Julie was, too.

"That's a desk, darling, not a foot stool," his mother said as she breezed in. She sat on the edge of said desk. "And it's an heirloom."

He smiled. His mother was the exact opposite of her father. Davis Roberts had had money, sure, but he'd kept a small house and lived modestly. Elise Roberts Carrington-Wright didn't know the meaning of modest. She and his dad had been perfectly matched—and perfectly unhappy. But his mom had a quirky sense of humor and a good heart underneath the diamonds and pearls.

"I'm surprised to see you, Mom." He stood to give her a kiss on her proffered cheek.

She cupped his face, the way she'd been doing for as far back as he could remember. "I could say the same. You're the one who's always gone. I'd hardly know you lived here."

"It could be because the house is palatial," he replied mildly. He and Alexis had moved back in after their dad had passed away two years ago. Their dad, in his traditional selfish way, had up and died in his mistress' bed. Elise had been understandably upset, just as much from her husband's death as the public embarrassment.

Moving back hadn't been a problem. The house was so large he could have an orgy in one wing and his mother wouldn't hear a peep of it. Not that he was into orgies. He was more of a one-woman kind of guy.

"You could hide yourself less when you're home." She looked around his office and wrinkled her nose. "Are you sure you wouldn't like me to redo this room? After Alexis's wedding, of course."

His sister's wedding was the current cause Elise was throwing herself into. "I like it the way it is."

"It's dark, like a man decorated it."

"Since I'm a man, I guess that's a good thing."

She hummed, obviously not convinced.

"Did you just come down here to talk to me about furniture?"

"No." She physically wilted. "I came to get a drink to help calm my nerves."

"What's wrong with your nerves?" he asked as he went to the wet bar to the side of the room.

"The wedding. You can't imagine how difficult it is to organize an event for four hundred people."

He wanted to point out that he was pretty sure

Alexis hadn't wanted that many guests, but he knew better. He just signed the checks and kept quiet.

"The florist had a hissy fit a couple days ago," his mother continued, nodding as he handed her a glass of the sherry she liked. "Today she emailed me to say she wasn't going to do the flowers for the wedding. Can you imagine the nerve? It's only three weeks away. How am I going to find a florist to do the wedding in such a short period of time?"

He thought of Julie, but there was no way he was going to subject her to his mother—not to work for her, in any case. He didn't want to kill the relationship before it'd even started. "I'm sure you'll find someone, Mom. You always handle it."

"I do, don't I?" She gave him a direct look that never boded well for him. "About the wedding. Have you asked someone to be your date yet?"

"I'm working on it." He was going to ask Julie, but even he had the sense to wait until after their first date—not because he was worried he wouldn't like her, but because his chances of success would be much higher.

He pictured Julie in a dress short enough to show off her legs, with her hair down and her lips glossy. He hadn't seen her legs, but he knew they'd be incredible. He was getting turned on thinking about her. So he stopped, because having dirty thoughts about his soon-to-be lover in front of his mom seemed plain wrong.

"Hmm." She nodded and sipped her sherry daintily.

"What does that mean?" he asked suspiciously.

"Nothing, darling. Don't stay up too late." She flashed a Cheshire smile as she glided out of his office.

"Don't even think about it, Mother," he called after her.

She waved over her shoulder. "Good night, darling."

He stared after her. He was better off not imagining what she was planning.

He took the card Julie gave him out of his pocket. It was after eleven—too late to call, but he couldn't stop himself from sending her a text. *Thinking of you. —Scott*

Two seconds later she called him. "You have nothing better to do on a Saturday night than think about a woman you just met?"

"I can only think of a better way of spending my night," he said with a grin.

"I'm surprised it's just one."

"I didn't want to scare you off."

She chuckled softly. "You're..."

"What?" he prompted, leaning back in his chair.

"Different," she replied.

"Not the most enthusiastic endorsement, but I'll take it." He set his glass on the desk. "Are you home?"

"I'm at my shop. I'm working on a pet project."

"At eleven o'clock on a Saturday night?"

"I don't have time to work on it during the day, so I do it after hours. I didn't mean to be here so late." She sighed. "It's not going well. I'm having trouble with the frame I'm building."

"I can come over and help," he offered.

"Are you an artist?"

"No, I'm a businessman, but I can be pretty motivating."

"I'm sure you can be," she said with a smile in her voice. "What sort of business?"

"I invest in business ventures. I back Nicole and her line."

"That's impressive."

"It sounds more impressive than it is, but I like it. I help people successfully launch their dreams, and I make a nice living doing it. I can't ask for more." Except someone to share it with him.

"You must be good at what you do."

"I'm very good," he said, the innuendo unmistakable.

She laughed softly. "Promises, promises."

"I always keep my promises." He felt alive and impatient with anticipation. "I'm looking forward to Monday night, Julie," he said softly.

"I am, too." She paused. "Truthfully, I'm tempted to invite you over now."

"To help you with your project?"

"To help me off with my jeans."

He shifted with the zing of desire her words caused. He wanted to say *yes* and that he'd be right over, but he knew the benefit of delayed gratification. He also didn't want to give her a reason to have regrets in the morning.

Reining in his impatience, he said, "Monday."

"Monday," she repeated, a promise in one word.

He'd take it—and her. Soon.

Chapter Four

*T*HREE MONTHS OF hard work was coming to a culmination in less than three weeks, and the only thing Julie could think about tonight was Scott, his talented lips, and their impending date tomorrow night.

She shook her head, staring at the design spread on her kitchen counter. She had too much riding on the competition to get distracted now.

The theme to this year's San Francisco Flower Competition was "San Francisco Spirit." A lame subject, in her opinion, but she wasn't going to criticize the committee.

Instead, she'd done her best to figure how to

symbolize it. What she'd come up with was brilliant: a to-scale representation of San Francisco's cityscape, done in a rainbow-assortment of flowers.

The thing was she'd been having trouble with the foundation for the panorama. The carved blocks didn't look enough like the San Francisco skyline. So last night she'd scrapped her previous design and started from scratch. She'd edited the designs one last time tonight, and she finally had it right. She hoped.

Her intercom buzzed. Knowing it was just Sophie, she buzzed her in.

Except saying "just Sophie" was an understatement. There was nothing that was "just" about Sophie Martineau. There were a million reasons why she was so successful, and most of all was her presence. When she walked into a room, everyone knew it.

Somehow, the world-famous actress had decided that she and Julie were soul mates. Secretly, Julie was grateful for Sophie's friendship and support. But she'd never tell that to the actress. Sophie already had an overinflated sense of self—compliments just made her unbearable.

Julie opened her front door as Sophie skipped up to the top landing.

"No wonder you're so thin," the actress said as she walked in, taking off her wrap and the sunglasses she wore night or day, to avoid being recognized. "I'd be a rail if I climbed up and down those stairs a couple times a day."

As if Sophie wasn't skinny as it was. *Actresses.* Julie shook her head.

Sophie dropped her things on the folded up futon and gave her a kiss on each cheek. "This date of yours is so exciting. Even Tony was beside himself when I told him."

"Right." Julie snorted. She knew better than to think that Sophie's husband, a big-time talent agent, cared one way or the other. "I'm sure he can't wait for a detailed report."

"He can't wait because *I* can't wait." Sophie gave her a smile cloaked in feminine satisfaction. "I have the man wrapped around my pinkie."

Her friend talked a good game, but Julie knew it was a two-way street. There wasn't anything Sophie wouldn't do for someone she loved, and she loved Tony in a way Julie didn't understand.

For some reason, Scott came to mind. Ridiculous, because she didn't know anything about him other than he had a PhD in oral gymnastics.

Before Sophie could pick up on her thoughts, Julie walked into her tiny kitchen. "Want something?"

"Do you have Perrier?" her friend asked, following her.

She gave Sophie a look from over the refrigerator door. "Seriously?"

The actress shrugged. "If you don't ask for what you want, you never get it. What is this?"

Getting out two bottles of water, she looked over her shoulder. "It's my design for the flower competition. I'm going to crush Dr. Hyacinth Gardner this year."

Sophie flipped a sheet. "Your animosity towards this woman might be construed as excessive by some people."

"Oh, it's really not." She set a water bottle on the counter and gestured as she uncapped her own. "I'm doing society a favor. That woman is a menace, and someone needs to take her down."

"And you're the perfect vigilante to do it?" Sophie asked in her dry way.

"Yes."

Her eyebrow arched.

Julie shook her head. "Don't look at me that way. She totally deserves it, and not because she's won the competition for the past five years, flaunts all her degrees, or calls herself 'the Dr. Oz of flora.'" All those were good reasons on their own. "She cheats, Sophie."

Her friend frowned, which she never did because it caused wrinkles. "You have proof of this?"

"No, but every year something goes wrong with my entry. One year, my Coit Tower replica died inexplicably. By the time the judges got to it, it looked like a post-apocalyptic decaying penis."

Sophie laughed. "Tell me you took pictures."

"Hell no. I wanted to forget." Julie crossed her arms, getting angry remembering it. "I thought I'd done something wrong, until a couple years of disasters later. Last year, my shipment of crimson carnations went missing, and I received white chrysanthemum instead."

"That's not so awful."

"It is if you're building the Golden Gate Bridge." She shuddered, picturing the pitying looks on the judges' faces.

Sophie propped herself against the counter. "Is her name really Dr. Hyacinth Gardner? Because if I had a florist character in a screenplay, I wouldn't name her something so obvious."

"I know, right?" She thought of Hyacinth's fake smile and crossed her arms. "I really can't stand her."

"Because she's evil, or because you're jealous?"

Maybe she was a little jealous of Hyacinth's degrees—she hadn't been able to afford to go to college—but this was about professional pride. She was a good florist with a prospering business. She should be able to win the trophy, degree or not.

"I didn't come here to analyze your psyche." Sophie set her water down and pushed off the counter. "Take me to your closet. We have a date outfit to strategize."

Julie sighed. Knowing better than to argue, she trudged to her small closet and opened the door. It was on the tip of her tongue to tell Sophie that it didn't matter what she wore — she planned on taking it off as soon as Scott arrived — but she didn't need to give her friend that kind of ammunition.

Sophie's nose wrinkled as she flipped through the few hangers in the closet. "Where's the rest of your wardrobe."

"In the dresser." She pointed to the three-drawer chest sitting on the closet floor.

Her friend gaped, her face a mask of horror. "I don't know whether to throw my arms around you and tell you I'll rescue you or to stage an intervention."

Julie rolled her eyes. "It's not a big deal. I'll just wear jeans."

"Oh, no, you won't." Sophie turned to her, a militant gleam in her eyes. "I'll bring you options tomorrow."

"I don't need options. It's just a quick date." She turned around so Sophie wouldn't read the lie and went to huddle in the corner of the futon. "I don't have time to get serious about anyone right now, anyway. I need to focus on the competition."

"And yet you agreed to go out with this man." Sophie followed and stood over her like a righteous Amazon. "What do you think that means?"

"That I need to see a shrink?"

Sophie grinned. "A love doctor might be more fitting."

"Love?" She recoiled physically. "Who said anything about love? We're getting together for pizza. End of story."

"Deny it all you want, but I saw the way you two looked at each other."

"How did we look at each other?" Julie asked in horrified fascination.

"Like you two could look at each other for the rest of your lives."

She thought about that. Then she shook her head. "You're just being dramatic."

Sophie pointed a red-tipped finger in her face. "If I'm right, I get to plan the wedding of the century for you."

Julie shuddered at the thought. "What if you're wrong?"

Her friend shrugged as she wrapped her shawl around her shoulders. "Then you lose."

She opened her mouth to argue, but she had a feeling Sophie was right.

Chapter Five

BULL PACED BACK and forth outside Nicole's *atelier*, as she called it.

In the past year, Nicole's life had changed. She'd married Griffin Chase, one of the best rock stars on the planet, if you asked Bull. They had bought a spacious condo in Laurel Heights, but she rented this space for working, to keep work and her private life separate.

He glanced at his watch. It was only nine in the morning—he wasn't even sure she'd be there yet. Her working schedule varied because Grif was a musician.

But he was at his wit's end. He'd tried to track

down Josephine Belle, but had no luck. There were a surprising number of women with that name, and none of them in San Francisco.

Normally, he would have been calmer about finding her. He liked unraveling mysteries. But the group taking his smoothie line national was dragging their feet with the contract, and one uncertainty in his upended life seemed more than enough at the moment.

It'd have been nice to have someone who cared at his back. Someone to share his frustrations with, who'd rub his head and tell him it'd all work out. Someone like Josephine Belle.

So he worked out, trying to burn off the frenetic energy on his own. Only it didn't help, because there was only one way he wanted to work it off: in bed, with Josephine.

The door suddenly flung open, and Nicole leaned against the lintel. "You coming in, or do you want to wear a groove in the hall?"

He growled under his breath—not at his friend, but at his situation—and strode into her workshop.

"You're cheery this morning," she said brightly as she closed the door. "I'm so glad you came to spread it here."

"You're lucky I love you." He walked into the airy, bright studio and thrust his hand out. "I brought you a smoothie. It's a new combination I'm trying out."

"Awesome. Your smoothies are always delicious." Smiling, she took it and rose on her toes to kiss his cheek. "Do the men you fight know what a big softie you are?"

"I'm not fighting anyone. I'm retiring," he blurted for the first time ever. He hadn't even told Ethan, his best buddy, yet.

Nicole's eyebrows lowered in concern. "You didn't get hurt, did you?"

"No." But it was only a matter of time. His

fights stayed with him longer these days, and he woke up sore more often than not. "I never wanted it to be my entire life. It was just a way to bide my time until I found what I wanted to do."

"What's that?" she asked as she perched on the stool at her drafting table.

He nodded at the to-go cup in her hand.

"Smoothies," she said, lighting up. "Of course. And then you can be your own spokesman, because who better than a popular, champion fighter? Are you opening your own shop?"

"I'm going into partnership to have them manufactured." At least that was the deal he wanted. The company backing him was being difficult on that point.

"That's so great!" She hopped up and gave him a big hug. "Do you have details on the deal?"

"I'm waiting for the final contract." As she resettled on her stool, he brought a chair closer, turned it around, and straddled it. "Basically I asked to oversee the product line and overall branding, but they handle all the grunt work and distribution for a cut."

"I didn't know you were working on this." She shook her head. "You've been very hush-hush. It has to have been a while. Deals like this don't happen overnight."

"It's not a done deal yet, and I didn't want to eclipse your achievements."

"You wouldn't have." She grinned proudly. "I *rocked* the lingerie show."

"You did." He cleared his throat. "About the show—"

"Yes?"

He frowned at the way she was batting her eyes at him. "If you know what I'm going to ask, you could just put me out of my misery."

"But this way is so much more fun." She laughed at his scowl.

"You don't have to look like you're enjoying it so much."

"What fun would that be?" She tipped her head. "This is about Joey, of course."

"She didn't want to go out with me," he grumbled, feeling like a surly bear.

Nicole patted his chest. "You'll just have to work harder at winning her over, won't you?"

"Damn straight. I need her address." He pointed at her. "That's where you come in."

"I can't give you her address," Nicole said regretfully. "Have you tried Googling her?"

"Yes, but I don't know her last name." He scrubbed the top of his head with his palm. "You'd think Josephine Belle would be uncommon enough, but it wasn't."

Nicole shook her head, but there was a gleam in her eyes. "I just can't give out personal information like that for my models, especially for *Josephine Williams*."

He perked up. "Josephine Belle Williams." Her whole name tasted delicious on his tongue, just like *she* would be.

Nicole nodded vehemently. "I can't give you her address or tell you that she works as a curator at the Asian Art Museum."

He stood, grabbed Nicole by the shoulders, and smacked a big kiss on her lips. *"Thank you."*

Nicole wiped off his affection with the back of her hand, but there was a grin on her face. "What's your plan?"

"I'm going to send her the corset."

Nicole's froze. "The corset you bought from Romantic Notions last year?"

"Of course. I've been looking for the woman who'll fit it, and I think she's Josephine Belle."

"That's your plan?"

He thought about the red corset, and about Josephine filling it out, and growled hungrily in his throat. "It's a great plan."

"Let me know how that goes for you," she said, her tone dripping in skepticism.

"You don't think I'm going to be successful," he stated.

"It depends. Are you going to invite her out to dinner a couple times before you pull out the corset?"

He made a face. "My Josephine Belle wouldn't appreciate that. She's a direct woman."

"You've got that part right," Nicole conceded. "But there are two flaws with your declaration."

"What?"

"That any woman wouldn't be freaked out by having some guy she doesn't know giving her lingerie, and that she's yours."

"She's not mine yet, but she will be."

"And the part about her being freaked out?"

"I'm giving her lingerie, not herpes."

Nicole didn't look convinced. "To some women, it'd be the same thing."

"Josephine Belle isn't the usual woman." He grinned and kissed his friend's cheek. He waved over his shoulder as he started to leave. "I've got high hopes. Wait and see."

Chapter Six

JULIE HEARD THE door to her flower shop ring. "Be right out," she shouted from the back store-room, juggling the bunches of Leonida roses she needed to prep for Mr. Raskin's weekly order to his wife. He sent her two dozen of the rust-tipped ivory roses every Monday since before Julie had started working in the flower shop as a teenager. It touched even Julie's sarcastic heart.

Was Scott a flower sender? She frowned as she kicked the refrigerator door shut. She had plenty of flowers—she didn't need more. All of those roman-tic trappings were lost on her. Sure, she encouraged other people to indulge in them—it was good for business—but she didn't believe in them for herself.

She was seeing him tonight.

A shiver of anticipation ran through her. She didn't need or want any props—she just wanted him.

Shifting the flowers in her arms, she hurried out onto the floor. "Sorry about tha—"

She stopped suddenly, stunned.

Dr. Hyacinth Gardner looked up, just as startled, from the front counter—the front counter where Julie had the San Francisco Flower Competition entry form.

"What the hell?" Glaring, Julie hurried forward and used the roses to cover up the papers. Her design plans weren't laid out—she'd only been filling out the form—but no way was she taking a chance.

"Hello, Julie." Hyacinth hitched her purse higher on her shoulder and gave her a sticky sweet smile that didn't reach her eyes. "I was in the neighborhood, so I thought I'd stop by and see how you're doing."

"I *was* doing great." She crossed her arms.

"Now I'm suddenly feeling sick to my stomach."

"I probably have something in my purse to help that."

"Like a poison apple?"

Hyacinth shook her head and tried to look mournful. "I don't know what I've done to deserve your enmity, but I'd like to bury the hatchet."

"I'm sure you would." Right in her back. Julie narrowed her eyes. "Are you done? Because I actually work for a living."

The woman sighed, like she was so misunderstood. She waved to the counter. "The offer still stands. If you need help with your design, let me know. You know I studied design in college. And since I've won so many years in a row, it's safe to say I'm dialed in to what the judges like."

Or that she's sleeping with them all. Julie shook her head. "I'll do this on my own."

Hyacinth shrugged. "If you change your mind, let me know. Good luck, Julie."

She watched until the woman was out the door, to make sure she actually left. Then she looked down at the counter. Maybe she should disinfect.

The door jingled open again. Her head snapped up, ready to tell Hyacinth to get out. But it was Sophie.

"As promised," Sophie announced, entering the flower shop like it was a scene and she was the leading lady.

For the first time, Julie noticed the piles of clothes in her arms. "Are you headed to make a donation at Goodwill?"

"These are outfit choices for your date tonight. We're going to play dress-me-up-Julie." She plopped them down on the worktable and then hopped up on the counter. "Take your clothes off."

Julie rolled her eyes as she picked up the roses for Mrs. Raskin. "If I had a dollar for every time someone walked into my shop and ordered me to strip."

"Come on." Sophie flashed her famous pout. "Are you going to deny me this pleasure? Close up the shop. I brought my makeup. We'll do a make-over."

"*No.*" She shook her head as she stuck the roses in a bucket of water. "No way. I'm not letting you anywhere near my face. He's going out with me, not a clown."

Sophie wilted like a week-old tulip.

"Fine. I'll wear one of the outfits you brought, but I draw the line there." It wasn't going to matter what she wore. She had a feeling she wasn't going to stay clothed long—if she were lucky. Not that she was going to tell Sophie that.

The pout faded instantly, and Sophie shrugged. "Baby steps, I guess. Where are you guys going?"

Julie shrugged, not wanting to admit he was coming over. "I don't know."

Sophie crossed her arms and gave her the imperious, queen of the world look she was so good at. "I know you're a private person and not used to sharing with others, but you're going to have to get over that, because I'm going to sit on you until you tell me all about your date with this guy. You know that, right?"

"You're insane. You know that, right?"

"Mad as a hatter. Keep me apprised." Sophie slipped off the counter and grabbed her in a tight hug. Julie pretended to flail for a moment before she gave in. Sophie gave the best hugs. But out loud, she said, "You do this just to harass me."

"Of course I do." Sophie flashed her world-famous smile as she let go. She slid her sunglasses on her face.

As she sashayed out of the shop, another woman walked in.

Laurel Heights was affluent. Part of the success of Back to the Fuchsia was its location. She'd lucked into that. She'd started working there as a teenager, when she'd stumbled upon the flower shop and fallen in love with the blooms. Because she'd had no money for college, she'd started working there full-time after high school. It'd been a no-brainer to buy the shop when the previous owner had decided to retire.

Laurel Heights was a far cry from the low-income neighborhood in San Leandro, where she'd grown up. Still, Julie had been there so long she was used to affluent-looking women walking into her shop.

But this woman was a cut above them all. She had a posh style that reeked breeding and luxury beyond the average Laurel Heights patron. Not a strand of her ash blond hair was out of place, and she had the flawless body of someone who paid to have it maintained. Julie checked to see if the woman was leaving a breadcrumb trail of hundreds in her wake.

When the lady took her sunglasses off, Julie saw that she was older than she'd expected. Her mother's age, though her mother had years of hard work lining her skin.

"Excuse me," the rich woman said in a soft, cultured voice. "I'd like to speak to Julie Miller."

"I'm Julie." It never boded well when they used your full name. She wiped her hands and stepped forward. "I own this shop."

The woman looked around, obviously evaluating. Then she nodded like she was satisfied. She turned to Julie, determination in her eyes. "My name is Elise Carrington-Wright."

Julie stilled, her breath caught in her throat. She wanted to ask if she was the socialite Elise Carrington-Wright, who sat on the judges' panel for the San Francisco Flower Competition, but she knew she didn't need to ask. There could only be one Elise Carrington-Wright, and this lady was obviously it.

She frowned. "I don't understand why you're here in my shop. You use Nancy Brighton typically."

The woman eyed her shrewdly. "You know that?"

Julie shrugged. "It's my business to know who's interested in flowers."

"Yet you haven't tried to woo me away from Nancy."

"I don't poach from other florists." Julie pursed her lips to keep from adding that she'd make an exception for Hyacinth Gardner.

The woman nodded, her expression set. "I knew you had to be good for my son to use your shop."

"Your son?"

"Prescott Carrington-Wright III," the woman replied, pride evident in her voice.

She didn't recall ever sending out flowers for the son, but maybe his assistant ordered them. It wasn't uncommon, and he sounded arrogant enough not to handle details like that himself.

Whatever. However this woman had found

her, Julie wasn't going to question it. "What can I do for you?"

"My daughter is getting married in three weeks, and I've decided not to use Nancy."

Julie raised her brows. "That means either you're high maintenance or that Nancy slacked on the job."

The woman gaped at her for a moment before she laughed a merry tinkle of amusement. "You don't mince words. No wonder my son likes your work. If he and Nancy are to be trusted, I'm definitely high maintenance. Nancy quit because we weren't seeing eye-to-eye on the arrangements. I like to think *she* was being difficult. I want what I want, and she wasn't listening to me. I'd like to hire you to do the job, if you think you can."

"There's no question about whether I can do it, and better than anyone." Julie shrugged. "When's the wedding?"

"In three weeks, on June 15th. I also need flowers for the bridal shower and rehearsal dinner. The bridal shower is in a week, and the rehearsal dinner is three days before the wedding."

It'd be a nice chunk of change. Not that Julie needed it—she lived modestly and the flower shop made a decent income. But having the Carrington-Wright wedding in her portfolio would be great.

The only thing was that the wedding fell on the day after the flower competition. Nothing was standing in the way of her winning this year—not even a high-profile wedding. Julia pursed her lips as she considered it. But if she did a couple things ahead of time and turned down other big orders, she could manage all of it.

She faced the socialite. "I should let you know that I'm entering the San Francisco Flower Competition."

Mrs. Carrington-Wright perked up. "Is that so? If you do the wedding, I'll be sure to put in a good word for you."

"*No.*" Julie shook her head vehemently. "That's exactly what I don't want."

The woman frowned. "I don't understand."

"I want to win on my own merit, not because I worked the system." She didn't want there to be any question why she won: because of her talent. When Hyacinth saw her holding up the trophy, Julie wanted the other women to be clear that Julie was the best. "So I don't want favors."

"You're so much like Prescott. Yet another reason he must patronize you." The socialite held her hand out. "Make me happy with Alexis's wedding and you can have whatever you want."

"You're on." Julie took it and sealed the deal.

Chapter Seven

GIVING UP ON any productivity, Scott gave his assistant the afternoon off and decided to go for a run, to burn off some of his excess energy before his date with Julie.

When he arrived at the family house, there were several vehicles in the circular drive. Figuring it was wedding hoopla, he pulled around to the back and slipped in from the kitchen entrance. With any luck he could avoid all of it.

Celeste, their cook, looked up as he walked through. He held a finger to his lips and winked at her. Grinning, she shook her head and went back to chopping carrots.

Running up the back stairs to his room, he changed into shorts, a T-shirt, and his favorite running shoes. Strapping his phone to his arm, he snuck out the same way he'd come in.

He was doing his pre-run stretches on a patch of lawn in the back yard when he heard the bushes on the edge of the property rustle. He stopped and looked as a long, jean-clad leg hitched over the side. Before he could say a word, a female form dropped into his yard with a loud "*Oof.*"

A female form he recognized. "Hello, KT," he said.

She pushed the long cascade of hair from her eyes and glared at him. "Don't say a frickin' word."

He shook his head. "I wasn't about to."

Grumbling, she stood up and brushed off her butt. "But you were thinking it."

"I know better." When she gave him the stink eye, he shrugged. "I have a sister."

"Humph." Frowning, she looked around,

as if waiting for guards to come haul her away.

"Are you in some sort of trouble?"

"Good guess, Sherlock. My mom is after me."

Her mom was Lara, one half of the legendary rock duo, Anson and Lara. It was bad enough having super-rich socialite parents like his—he couldn't imagine growing up as the eldest daughter of a power couple like Anson and Lara. Her parents weren't just world famous, they were a force. It wasn't any wonder she tended to hide in the shadows, even more so because music was her passion. Her sister Bijou, also a performer, was much more outgoing.

"What did you do?" he asked, stretching his quads.

"Nothing, which is why she's after me." He must have looked confused, because she sighed and said, "She invited some dude over to meet me. Like, as a date."

"Ah." He nodded. "She's being a mom."

"Exactly." She tugged down her jacket and stuck her hands in the pockets. "Well, I don't want to keep you from your run. I'm going to find a dark hole to hide in for the next twenty years until she decides that I'm a lost cause and gives up trying to find me a mate."

"I hate to tell you this"—he leaned in—"but they never give up."

"Damn it," she said with feeling. "I was afraid of that. Can I take refuge in my usual spot?"

He smiled. "Do you think she'll give up any time soon, or will I have to keep you for a while?"

"Is that an option?" KT looked at him hopefully.

Laughing, he squeezed her arm. "Celeste is in the kitchen."

KT perked up. "I love Celeste."

"You love her cookies." He swiped his phone to turn his music on and turned on his Bluetooth earphones. "You sure you don't want to go for a run with me?"

She looked at him, horrified. "And let Celeste down? No, thank you."

He grinned as he watched her head for the back door. KT had been hiding in his house for as long as he could remember. They'd met in this very spot, when she'd been a gangly seven year old crawling through the hedges, even then trying to escape her mother. Unlikely as it seemed, over the years, the brash musician had become one of his closest friends.

He had KT to thank for meeting Julie, because KT had been the one to give him the tip about Nicole and her lingerie endeavor. It seemed Griffin Chase, Nicole's boyfriend, and KT were good friends.

KT had been trying to help Nicole, but she'd really done Scott the bigger favor. He'd gotten to invest in a positive business that enhanced women's self-images, because Nicole's lingerie was geared toward making all women feel beautiful, and he met the love of his life.

He shook his head at the insanity and set out for his run.

An hour and a half later when he returned, he reentered from the kitchen, in case there were still matrimonially charged women around. He looked for KT on his way to his suite, but she was either buried deep in the bowels of his house or back at her own place.

In his room, he stripped off his sweaty clothes and took a shower. He redressed in casual clothing, checked his email, and ordered a pizza for their date.

For most women, he'd go to the cellar and pick out a bottle of champagne to take, too, but Julie didn't seem like a champagne girl. So he picked up a six-pack of a rare Highland ale he thought she might enjoy, and along with the pizza, he drove to the address she'd given him.

She lived in the inner Richmond, above a Chinese restaurant. He pressed the number for her apartment, pushing open the door when it buzzed.

When he reached the top floor, he saw her leaning in the doorway, and felt like he'd reached the pot of gold at the end of the rainbow. She wore jeans that hung low on her hips and a sweater. Her feet were bare, her hair was in a ponytail, and it didn't look like she had any makeup on.

She was gorgeous.

She gave the pizza box a cursory glance before returning her gaze to him. "You're punctual."

"I was eager."

The corner of her mouth kicked up. "I like eager. Come in."

He walked inside, but instead of an apartment, he felt like he stepped into a tropical forest. It was warm and lush, with plants and orchids everywhere.

Then he noticed the futon in the middle of the room, unfolded and beckoning, covered in a fluffy comforter with two pillows at the head.

He stopped in his steps. "That makes a statement. I just hope it's the statement I imagine it is."

"Probably." Julie took the pizza and beer from his hands. "It seemed pointless to fold it away."

"I knew you were clever." Before she could get away, he reached out for her and kissed her, just like he'd been imagining since the night at the lingerie show. It felt just as hot, and even deeper with the promise of futon thrown in.

"I should put this stuff down before I drop them," Julie said against his lips.

"Hurry." He let go of her and watched her walk into the attached kitchenette. It was a small studio, but it was amazingly homey. "I like your place."

She gave him an incredulous look. "I asked you if you were a serial killer, but I should have asked if you'd sustained any brain damage in your life."

Chuckling, he shrugged out of his jacket and

hung it on the front door knob. "I'm not saying it's not small. I'm saying I like it."

"Well then, I guess I can't question your sanity," she said with a dry smile. "Do you want a beer?"

"I want you."

Julie met his gaze, her cheeks flushed, and rejoined him. "Okay," she said as she wound her arms around his neck.

He wrapped his arms around her waist and squeezed her to him, burying his face in the crook of her neck. "I've been waiting for this for so long."

She nodded. "All weekend."

"All my life," he corrected as he lifted her chin and kissed her again.

She moaned against his mouth, her leg hitching on the back of his knee, pulling him closer. "This is a first for me," she murmured.

He smiled against her lips. "Sex?"

She grinned back. "Yes."

"You don't kiss like a virgin," he said, nibbling her lips.

"That's because I'm not." She threaded her fingers in his hair and looked up at him. "I don't bring random guys over. Ever."

"I'm not a random guy."

"No, you're not." She began to unbutton his shirt.

He let her push it off his shoulders, helping her when the cuffs caught on his wrists. Reciprocating, he lifted her T-shirt over her head and paused. "You don't have a bra on."

"And you're astute." She unbuckled his belt.

"I'm incredibly turned on, is what I am." He ran a finger over the puckered tip of her pert breast. "I like your outfit."

"My friend tried to dress me up," she said as she undid his pants, "but it seemed pointless since we were staying in."

"This may be forward and perhaps too soon," he said as he slid his hands in front to undo her jeans. "But I should warn you that I'm going to ask you to marry me."

"Uh-huh," she said as she unbuttoned the waistband of his pants.

He stopped her hands and waited until she looked up at him. "I mean it."

Her brow furrowed. "What have you been smoking, and why haven't you offered to share?"

"I'm serious, Julie." He took her chin. "Not today or tomorrow, but soon enough. You better wrap your mind around it so that you're ready to say yes when I do."

"But I don't know anything about you." She watched as he unzipped her jeans. "I mean, what do you do for a living? Do you do dishes? Listen to Meatloaf on high volume?"

"I'm an investor. I'm happy to do dishes. And,

no, I'm not a fan of Meatloaf." He kissed her, sliding his hands inside her underwear and gripping her from behind.

"Do you expect someone to cook for you all the time? Because you should be warned that I'm not domestic."

"We'll order in."

"How do you take your coffee?"

"Black." Before she could ask her next question, he said, "I like to run, and I like to listen to jazz. Friends are important, and so is family. My mom drives me insane, but I feel lucky to have her. I love my sister, and not just because she makes me money. I'd much rather go to a dive spot than a Michelin-starred restaurant."

"That's a good start, but we're talking marriage." Julie wiggled her hips to help shimmy her pants and underwear down and stepped out of the legs. "What if you squeeze the toothpaste from the middle? Or leave your shoes all over the living room so I trip on them all the time?"

"We'll work on those things." Then he held her face to look her in the eyes. "Just tell me you aren't completely against the idea."

She shook her head, seeming dazed. "No, not completely against it, even if it's completely mad."

"I can work with that." He kissed her again, backing her up until she tumbled onto the futon. Then he quickly got out of the rest of his clothes and followed her down.

Chapter Eight

THE ONLY THING she could think of as he stripped out of his clothes was that he wanted to marry her. No one had ever wanted to marry her before.

She'd never been tempted to marry anyone.

If it were any other guy, she'd have known he was just giving her lines. But Scott truly wasn't any other guy, and she'd already agreed to have sex with him. He had no reason to give her lines—he was guaranteed to get lucky without any promises.

Quite frankly, the way he'd looked at her when he'd made the statement was enough to show her that he meant every word.

Mind boggling.

He climbed over her. There was something serious and real in his eyes as he slid up her body. When he blanketed her, he framed her face with his hands. "I don't walk up to just any random woman and kiss her the moment I meet her."

She arched her brows. "It's a strange time to tell me this, isn't it? When you already have me naked?"

"I want you to understand where I come from and who I am." He began kissing his way down her neck as he talked. "My grandfather told me when I met the right woman, I'd know. He was right."

"How did you know?" she asked, twining her fingers in his hair.

"The kiss, and a gut reaction. The same way I know a good investment when I hear it." He ran a light hand over her breasts, tracing the curve at her side. "I like to take risks, but I'd never risk something this important, which is why I wanted to lay my cards out on the table."

Goosebumps rose on her skin wherever he touched her. "Are you telling me this deliberately while your hands are driving me crazy?"

"Are my hands driving you crazy?" he asked with a devilish grin.

"You know I want more." She narrowed her eyes. "I had the futon open."

"What do you want?" Watching her, he trailed his hand down her ribcage to the hipbone. "This?"

She took his hand and put it between her legs, where she was burning for him. "That."

"That, I can do." He tested her with a finger, parting her outer lips and dipping in.

Sharp shocks of pleasure shot through her, and she inhaled sharply, gripping his hair tighter. "It's not enough."

"Still?" He caressed her more firmly, a slow, gasp-rending drag that made her break out in a sweat. She squeezed her eyes shut, her head swimming, like she'd had too much to drink.

"Do you still want more?" he asked, his voice low and hungry.

"Yes." She cried out as he focused his touch. "*No.*"

"Which is it, Julie?" He scooted down, kissing her belly as he slid down. "I can stop."

"Don't you dare." She wanted more but wasn't sure she could take it.

"Just hold on," he told her as he replaced his fingers with his tongue.

The first lick had her jolting off the bed. She gripped his hair, sobbing in pleasure as his tongue worked its magic.

She was going to pass out, she realized as colors began to swim behind her eyelids. She gulped air, trying to calm herself, but it'd been a while, and he knew exactly where to touch her.

And then his lips closed over her and he sucked.

She came off the bed again, her body jackknifing with the force of her climax. She heard someone scream but it took her a moment to realize it was her own.

Scott rose and covered her again. She felt the coolness of the condom he'd managed to put on as he slowly inched his way in.

She pulled his mouth closer to hers. "This is *nice*."

He kissed her, a thorough exploration that left her even more breathless. "Your word choice leaves a little to be desired."

"I'm a florist, not a writer." She wrapped her thighs around his waist. "Are you going all in, or what?"

"I love the romance in your soul," he said with an amused grin, right before he plunged in.

Her hips arched of their own accord, as if she'd lost control of her body.

"Julie?" he whispered in her ear. "I'm all in."

There was subtext that went beyond the physical. She felt like she was drowning in so many ways, so she clung to him and held on as he steadily plunged into her. Every brush of his pelvis against her left her panting until she was positive she was going to pass out.

Suddenly the rhythm changed, slowing, going even deeper.

She ground her hips against him, feeling her climax build. Head falling back, she grabbed his back. "If you stop I'll kill you with my garden sheers."

"I won't stop until you come"—he slid a hand under her and tipped her hips up — "and even then I may keep going."

The angle changed, and the electric feelings intensified. Inside her, she felt him harden even more, ready himself, and that pushed her over the edge. As she cried out, so did he.

He didn't stop until the last tremor shot through her. Then he collapsed on top of her, both of them breathing heavily.

Scott spoke first. "You scratched my back. I think that means this was a success."

She chuckled, hooking her ankles over his calves. "It was nice."

He lifted his head and squinted at her. "Now *I* may threaten you with your garden sheers."

"Do you have the energy?"

"To do anything but lie here?" He shook his head. "No."

Stroking his chest, she said, "I liked it. It was like a cherry topping my day."

"Tell me about your day, darling." He propped his head on his palm.

"I got a really great client." She smiled as she thought about the coup of snagging the Carrington-Wright wedding. "I was worried about taking the event on since it overlaps with this competition I'm entering, but I decided to look at it as a challenge."

"What sort of competition?"

"Floral sculptures."

"Sexy," he deadpanned.

She smacked his shoulder. "I want to win."

"Of course you do."

"I'm going to, too." She kissed him, suddenly and without inhibition. "Are you hungry?"

"Starving."

She grinned, knowing he wasn't talking about food. She kissed him again before getting up to bring the pizza box back to the bed. Sitting cross-legged next to him, she opened the box and handed him a napkin. "I've never had pizza naked before."

He ran a hand along her thigh. "Then we should set a new naked pizza tradition."

"I'm down with that." She smiled and accepted the slice he offered her.

Chapter Nine

"So." Elise Carrington-Wright sat primly on the couch in her Pacific Heights home, not unlike a queen, holding court for her subjects. "While we're waiting for my daughter Alexis to join us, let me tell you what I'm thinking."

Julie mentally groaned. Brides' mothers were always a headache. She shifted on the uncomfortable chair she'd plopped on and pulled out her notebook. "Go ahead."

"A sea of white. It's an evening wedding, and the white will look stunning with the candles."

"True." Especially in this house.

Although to call this *a house* was a gross understatement. It might even be too big to qualify as a mansion. She was sure there were smaller castles in the world. The "house" sat on top of Pacific Heights, was four stories tall, had a circular drive, and a large fountain in front.

The Carrington-Wrights also had staff. Since Julie had arrived ten minutes ago, she'd come into contact with three servants. One looked like a butler. She didn't realize people still employed butlers.

"Maybe orchids for the wedding, and something less formal for the rehearsal dinner," Elise said as she poured tea for the two of them. She set Julie's cup on the table in front of her. "We should have daytime flowers for the bridal shower."

"Daytime flowers." She managed to repeat it without sneering. What the hell did that mean?

Rich people. She shook her head as she made a couple notes, thinking about what was in season and what she'd seen that could be unique. "What sort of budget am I working with here?"

Elise gave her a flat look. "We're Carrington-Wrights."

"Of course," she murmured, ducking her head so the socialite wouldn't see her roll her eyes.

A woman about Julie's age strode into the room. She was casually dressed in yoga pants, a workout top, and flip-flops. Her dark hair was clipped back at the sides, waving halfway down her back. She wore minimal makeup and had the largest diamond Julie had ever seen on her ring finger. It was amazing that the woman could even lift her hand, the rock was so big.

"Hello, I'm the bride," she said cheerily, extending her hand. "Alexis."

Julie shook it, squinting at the woman. She looked awfully familiar. "Have we met before?"

"Do you do exercise videos?" Alexis asked, sitting down next to her mother.

"Not if I can help it."

The woman laughed, a happy sound that made

Julie smile. "A lot of my customers feel that way."

"I was just telling Julie what we wanted for the wedding," Elise said calmly, handing her daughter a cup of tea.

Alexis groaned. "Did you tell her I wanted orchids? Because I really don't."

"Alexis, don't be unreasonable."

"I don't think it's unreasonable to have what I want for my own wedding." She faced Julie. "I'd like stephanotis flowers. Mother believes they're gaudy, but they're beautiful and modern, just like me."

Julie's lips quirked. She liked Alexis. Normally she'd have told Elise that it was Alexis's wedding and that she should have what she wanted, but she also wanted to make sure Elise had a positive impression of her. It wouldn't do to piss off a flower competition judge. "Maybe we can do some sort of mix."

Elise gave her a flat look.

"Or not," Julie muttered. She turned to Alexis. "Orchids really are classic."

"And I'm so *not*." She frowned at her mom. "Are you really going to be difficult about this?"

"I'm not the one being difficult, darling," Elise said with a raised brow.

Julie bit her tongue to keep quiet. It wasn't in her nature to butt out, especially where flowers were concerned. She had opinions and wasn't afraid to state them. Stephanotis were a better call — more unique — but Alexis wasn't the one she needed to please here. She didn't want an undue advantage in the competition, but she didn't want to shoot her herself in the foot either.

Still, she tried a different tactic. "Maybe I should come back later, after you two decide what you want."

"I know what I want." Elise gave her a look. "We are going to have orchids."

Alexis threw her hands in the air. "I'm not

sure why you needed me here if you're going to do whatever you want, despite my input."

"You're the bride, darling. You have to be involved."

Alexis faced Julie with an I-love-her-but-she's-impossible look.

Julie wasn't going to get involved in this discussion even though she knew Alexis was right on so many levels. She pulled out one of her albums. "I brought a portfolio of pictures form previous events. Of course, whatever I do will be unique, different than what I'll show you, but it'll give you an idea of what I'm thinking."

Elise held out her jeweled hand for the album. She flipped through the pages, her focus hawk-like. Alexis reclined and inspected her nails.

Julie pointed to the photo Elise landed on. "That's most like what I was thinking for the wedding, but with orchids of course."

The woman nodded and flipped the page.

When she reached the end of the book, she flipped backwards to another page. "And something in this vein for the bridal shower. For the rehearsal dinner let's go understated, like this."

Julie leaned to look at the photo, making a mental note that she was going to need to put in an order for cream white peonies.

Elise turned to her daughter. "What do you think, darling?"

Alexis shrugged. "Whatever you want, Mom."

Her mother obviously didn't like that answer, because her perfect nose wrinkled. "This is your wedding, Alexis."

"Which is why three hundred and fifty people I don't care about were added to the guest list?" she asked with a lift of her eyebrow.

Elise waved her hand dismissively. "We're Carrington-Wrights. We have social obligations. Speaking of social obligations, has your brother confirmed his date for your wedding?"

"He said he was working on it."

Elise nodded, her expression calculating.

"I don't like that look, Mother," Alexis said, and Julie had to agree.

"There is no look," Elise said with deceptive casualness. "I'm just going to work on it as well. Prescott needs a little encouragement sometimes."

"You know he hates it when anyone meddles in his life."

"I'm his mother, darling. I earned the right to meddle after nine months of pregnancy and two years of changing diapers."

Alexis shook her head. "I totally understand why people elope."

Elise turned to Julie. "The bridal shower is next week, and the rehearsal dinner is three days before the wedding. Perhaps you can send some ideas for bridal bouquets as well? Alexis wants something dramatic and large."

"Or a small bunch of pink daisies," her daughter said as she reached for a cookie. "You know, if anyone cares about my opinion."

Julie wanted to say she cared, but she reminded herself of the big trophy and smiled politely. Hopefully she didn't look like she was going to puke. "I'll get on that and send you some thoughts."

"Fabulous." Elise stood and shook her hand. "Thank you, Julie. I have a good feeling about this."

If only she did, too.

The feeling that she'd let down Alexis followed her all day, so when Scott stepped into her shop that afternoon, at first she just pouted at him.

"You don't look happy to see me," he observed as he closed the door. "Is this a bad time?"

She set the lilies she was holding in a bucket of water and walked around the worktable. "Not if you come here and kiss me."

"I can do that."

She sighed, instantly happier the moment his lips touched hers. She wrapped her arms around him and pressed closer.

"I've been thinking about this all day," he said between kisses. "I've *needed* this all day."

"You had a hard time focusing on work too?"

"I had a hard time, period." He brushed her hair out of her face, his hand trailing to her neck. "I was in a meeting, and I started thinking about you so when everyone got up to leave I had to wait unless I wanted to embarrass myself."

She chuckled, feeling the tension ease under his massaging fingers. "That'd be inconvenient."

"You have no idea." He lifted her chin. "Tell me you were just as bad."

She nodded, her throat oddly full of emotions. "I have a wedding I'm doing and I kept putting myself in the bride's place."

"Are you wearing underwear under your wedding gown?"

She laughed. She could feel his heart beating against her chest, and it was oddly peaceful. She snuggled closer and sighed. "Thank you."

"You feel better?" he asked, stroking her hair.

"Definitely."

"Want to tell me what happened?"

She sighed again. "I let the bride down by siding with her mother. I never do that, not unless the bride is insane."

"This bride was somewhat sane, I guess."

"I actually liked her. That's unheard of." She lifted her head to look at him. "Have you ever compromised your beliefs in business? To get something you wanted."

He gazed at her steadily. "I try to stay true to what I believe is right, but that said, you do what you need to do in order to achieve your objectives. It's business."

She pursed her lips as she thought about that. "I didn't really do anything but stay out of an argument between my client and her daughter."

"My mother and sister combat all the time." He grinned ruefully. "It's generally accepted that Mom wins."

"There wasn't even anything to win. It was only a difference in taste. Neither choice was bad."

"So then there really was no problem, right?"

"I guess." But there was, because normally she would've said something to support Alexis and she didn't.

"In any case, there's nothing you can do now, is there?" He took her hand. "Will it hurt business if you close early today? I have a craving for one of the almond croissants at Grounds for Thought."

"Let's go." She grabbed her coat and flipped the lights off. As she locked the door, she said, "I never play hooky."

"Ever?" Scott took her hand and led her away.

"I don't usually have a reason to. Besides, I

love work." She glanced at him. "When I was a kid, I wanted to be an artist."

"But you didn't pursue that?"

She shook her head. "I was awful at drawing. Picasso cringed from beyond the grave at my paintings. But I discovered I had a strange talent for putting flowers together and making them look like something more than a handful of weeds. More than that, I loved doing it. Go figure."

"I wanted to be a garbage man when I was a kid," he said as he opened the door to the café.

"No, you didn't." She grinned at him.

"I loved the trucks." He led them to the counter, his hand on the small of her back. "Want to choose a table while I order?"

"Sure." She picked a small, round table in the back corner, where there were two high-backed chairs. She didn't know Eve, the owner of the café, well, but Julie figured the woman wouldn't care if she moved the table and rearranged the chairs closer. Eve was always so sunny and pleasant—it was hard imagining her getting bent out of shape about anything.

She sat and watched Scott charm the barista. Some people wielded their magnetism like a weapon—like Sophie. Julie could tell Scott was just being friendly. It didn't hurt that he was so attractive.

He joined her, hands full with cups and plates. "I got an almond croissant. How could I not? It's my favorite. But I also got a chocolate one, because I was assured it'd make me feel like I was in Paris."

She smiled at his enthusiasm as he sat down. "Do you want to be in Paris?"

"Will you be there?" He slid a tiny cup of espresso close to her.

"I've never been to Paris." She picked up the coffee and sipped. Bitter. Trying not to make a face, she set it back down.

"I have a love-hate relationship with Paris," he said as he cut both croissants into smaller pieces. "When I arrive there, I can't remember why I go. The trip is long, the people are hard to crack, and it's crowded. But then I take a nap and visit my favorite *patisserie* for an almond croissant. I talk to the baker about how his children have grown, and he slips a strawberry tart in my bag when his wife isn't looking, and then I remember why I love it there."

She tried to imagine, but she had no frame of reference beyond her impression of Paris from movies. Actually, she'd never even been outside California.

"I'd love to show Paris to you." He offered her some of the pastries. "You'll love the *Musée d'Art Moderne de la Ville de Paris*, and there's a tiny restaurant in St. Germaine that I want to take you to. And you have to see the *Jardins des Plantes*, of course."

"Of course," she murmured, even though she didn't understand half of what he said.

He took her hand. "We'll stroll down the Seine at night, and stop for ice cream at Berthillon. Do you like ice cream?"

She shrugged, playing with the piece of croissant in her hand. She tried to imagine herself there, walking wherever it was he said, but she couldn't. The only place she could see herself was in her shop, snipping the ends of flower stalks. "It sounds like you know Paris really well."

"I go there pretty often, mostly for business but I always manage to sneak a little pleasure in." He winked at her.

Realizing she was making a total mess, she put the bit of pastry she was decimating back on the plate. She tried to smile back, but she felt oddly disconnected from him.

She didn't travel. She didn't dress nicely. She didn't wear an obviously expensive watch like he did. Her haircuts came from her garden sheers when her bangs became too long, not a fancy salon. She'd never had a manicure, and neither had she ever owned a passport. "Are you sure about this?" she blurted.

"This?" he asked, his brow furrowing. "Do you mean us?"

"It's just"—she bit her lip, wanting him so badly that she really didn't want to point out how different they were—"I don't travel much. I have my shop."

"I understand." His thumb caressed her palm. "It's your passion. But maybe I can convince you to take a few days here and there with me. I'll make it worth your while."

She hummed noncommittally.

He sobered. "You're serious. Are you having second thoughts about us?"

"It just seems like we're on separate paths in life."

"And paths converge." He leaned toward her, conviction in his direct gaze. "Julie, I meant it when I said I wanted to marry you. I know we're different, but we connect. Don't tell me you don't feel it."

"I do, but—"

"The rest is unimportant." He squeezed her hand. "I know we're going to have to make compromises to make this work, but what's important here is you and me. This doesn't happen every day."

"This?" she asked.

"This." He tugged her forward and kissed her.

The kiss whispered through her, soft but strong. It pushed all her misgivings into deep, dark corners, leaving only the crazy desire that he sparked in her.

"Take me home with you, Julie," he said softly, nuzzling her cheek. "We'll make love, and order Indian food later, and let it get cold as we make love again. I'll show you how you were meant for me, and how I'm meant for only you."

Shivering at the desire heavy in his voice, she nodded. She stood up, brushing at the crumbs on her jeans with her free hand. "But I'd like it stated for the record that I tried to talk reason into you."

He smiled as he shook his head. "There is no reason to this."

"You're saying it's madness?"

"The only thing mad here is how I feel about you."

"*That,* I can't argue with." She kissed him softly, hoping it wasn't foolish to feel so reassured. "Take me home and do me."

Chuckling, he led her out of the café. "You're so romantic. It's no wonder you're a florist."

"You'll think I'm doubly romantic when you see that I'm not wearing underwear."

He stopped so suddenly she almost ran into him. She grinned, wondering if she should tell him she'd just forgotten to do laundry. But the hungry look on his face changed her mind. It was working for him—she didn't want to spoil that.

So she tipped her head and motioned to the exit. "Want to come?"

"Yes, *please*."

She laughed as she led him home.

Chapter Ten

Bull sat at the bar in Absinthe, his fingers drumming the bar top, his drink untouched.

He'd sent Josephine Belle the corset.

He'd included a note to ask her to meet him at this restaurant. The bar was nice, and it was close to the Asian Art Museum, where she worked. Most of all, it was public and neutral, so she should have fewer qualms about meeting him there.

Whether she'd show up or not was the question.

He flexed his fingers, sore from the punching bag he'd beaten up that morning. He'd needed the workout after the phone call from his lawyer.

The first draft of the contract he'd received for his smoothie line wasn't in his favor in any way, but it was a negotiation.

Just like this thing with Josephine Belle was. Only she was touchier than the businessman he was dealing with, so he had to tread carefully. He didn't want to push her — at least not too much.

Nicole would argue that sending the corset was "pushing." He disagreed. It was setting up the game, which he intended on winning. He could see Nicole shaking her head, but he had to make a bold move. Sending a woman who didn't know him a scarlet red corset and panties was pretty bold.

How had she received the package? With surprise definitely. Probably with trepidation, too, because he could tell she was a cautious woman. He wasn't entirely certain she'd show up.

As long as she didn't throw it in his face, which was a distinct possibility and one he hoped to keep from happening. He wasn't sure how yet, but he knew he'd figure it out.

He looked at his empty hands. He thought of bringing her flowers, or a smoothie, or chocolate. In the end, he decided all of that was filler. He was the real draw here. He just hoped she thought that, too.

The restaurant's door opened. Bull looked up, hopeful but still shocked when he saw her enter.

She looked glorious.

She wore a dress that should have looked demure, with the hem down to her knees and covered by a short jacket. It hugged her curves and made his fingers twitchy to grab a hold of them. Her shoes had gray polka dot heels that made her calves look juicy. He sat up straight, humming deep in his throat.

Heels clacking with angry purpose, she strode toward him, a package in her hands. Her eyes were filled with passion. Yes, he'd have preferred it if that passion were more sexual and less murderous, but he'd take whatever she was willing to give him for the time being.

She yanked the barstool next to him and perched daintily on top. She set the package in front of him. "This is *highly* inappropriate."

She sounded like an incensed Southern Belle, and he couldn't help grinning. "I haven't even begun to show you inappropriate."

Before he could continue with that train of thought, the bartender sidled over. "Get you something to drink?"

Josephine looked disdainfully at his Sazerac. "A soda water, please."

"And a gin gimlet for my date," Bull added. "More tart than sweet, just like her."

"Got it." The bartender flipped a metal shaker in the air and started making the cocktail.

"I'm not your date." Josephine glared at him. "And you *aren't* cute."

"No, but I prefer to be called studly, anyway."

Bull nodded to the package, which presumably was the corset. "So did you try it on?"

"Of course not." Her adorable nose lifted in righteous indignation. The bartender set her drink in front of her and she picked it up and chugged down a hefty gulp.

Bull leaned forward. "Try it on. What do you have to lose?"

"My mind!" she exclaimed. She leaned forward and lowered her voice. "I know what you're doing."

"And what's that, sweetheart?" He tried not to look down her blouse.

Okay, just one peek — and it was delicious.

She lifted his chin with a finger. "I will *not* date a crazy man."

"Of course not. You'll date *me*."

"And you're crazy."

He crossed his arms. "What are you talking about, woman?"

"Look at you." She waved her hand in his general direction.

He looked down at himself. Today he'd worn a pair of slacks and a patterned long sleeved shirt. Although he rolled up the sleeves—he couldn't stand being bound in any way, and cuffs and collars were the worst. His shoes were polished and he was wearing the snazzy Gucci watch he'd bought when he'd won his first championship title. His head was freshly shaved, and he just had a facial a couple days ago. "I look good."

She rolled her eyes. "You do not. You look like a hoodlum dressed up as a playboy."

"I'm not a playboy, although I can see why you'd think I am, because of my incredibly good looks and suave demeanor." He shrugged. "It's an honest mistake to make, but I'm really a good ole boy from corn country."

She gaped at him. "There's nothing corn country about you. You've got a bald head and a thing on the side of your face."

"Thing?" He touched the UV tattoo he'd gotten in Amsterdam years ago after a particularly bloody grudge match, which he'd won, of course. "Are you disparaging the dandelion?"

"Is that what it is?" she asked in complete hauteur.

He pointed to his temple. "You know you want to kiss it."

"I do not." She looked horrified at the thought.

"Come on, sweetheart. Blow on it for good luck."

Her eyes narrowed. "Now you're goading me on purpose."

"Well, yeah, because you're making a judgment about something you know nothing about." He crossed his arms and sat back. "You ever think maybe it symbolizes something?"

She looked at it, her face set in a stubborn frown, but he could see the wheels turning in her head. "What does it symbolize?" she asked reluctantly.

"The ability to go with the flow regardless of where you end up." He frowned at her. "Aside from that, it's pretty. You work in an art museum. You should appreciate art."

She shook her head. "That's…"

He waited for her to finish her statement with *not art*, which was exactly what she was thinking. But she just shook her head again and clammed up.

"So you don't like it," he said.

"It's not a matter of whether I like it or not. It's on your *face*." She pointed at it. "Do you know who has tattoos on their faces? Criminals and people who never expect to pay taxes. You'll never be gainfully employed. No one hires people with tattoos on their faces, even if it's like yours."

"Why would I want to be employed?" He

knew he had to get on with the next phase of his life, because he couldn't continue to get pummelled on a regular basis and expect to live into his old age and be lucid, but his smoothie business was where it was at. He'd never even considered getting a job. His father would fly out and smack him upside the head if he as much as considered it. They were entrepreneurs in his family, not grunts.

Josephine groaned, putting a hand to her forehead. "You aren't employed, are you?"

"Of course I am." He scowled at her. "Are you saying I look like a hoodlum *and* a slacker?"

"What do you do?" she asked, ignoring his indignation.

"I told you I'm Kelly 'the Bull' Torres." He waited for recognition to light her beautiful face, but she just looked confused. "I'm an MMA fighter. You've never heard of me?"

"What's MMA?"

He gaped at her for a full ten count. Then he

shook his head. "I just don't know what to say, woman."

"Stop calling me that."

"Why? You look all woman to me." He looked her up and down, appreciating what he could see, even though the bar and her clothes hid a lot of the good parts.

"I don't understand you," she said, her cheeks flushing fetchingly.

He leaned forward. "There's only one thing to understand. I bought that corset for the woman I wanted to spend my life with, and I think you're it."

Her eyes widened with a combination of wariness, distrust, and fear. "You don't even know me!"

"So tell me about you. What's your favorite color, buttercup?"

Josephine glared at him. He wondered if he'd be able to hear her teeth grinding if he leaned —

closer. "That's not what I'm talking about," she said through her gritted teeth.

"Then tell me what you're talking about."

"I won't do crazy anymore," she exclaimed, throwing her arms in the air.

People around them hushed, staring. Bull smiled at them reassuringly. "It's all good, folks. She's on meds now."

"See?" she hissed, waving her arm. "This is what I'm talking about."

"What?" He leaned closer, mostly so he could inhale her scent. It was delicious. *She* was delicious. He couldn't wait to take a big bite out of her.

"I'm done dating crazy." She met him halfway, her amazing eyes trained on him. "Every guy I've ever dated has been insane. Always." She lifted one finger. "My first boyfriend in junior high, Danny Mosley, liked to rip wings off of flies and watch them flail. Jimmy Smith, in high school, liked to borrow my dresses. In college there was Marko, who was sensitive and liked to write music, mostly about me and my *attributes*."

Bull grinned. "I can't blame him. Your attributes are fine."

She glared at him. "Then there was Atticus Reginald. Enough said about him. A bunch of others followed, ending with Hershel."

"You dated a Hershel? Shouldn't that have been a warning sign in itself?"

"He was a cop, who seemed normal and down to earth until I found out he was tapping my phone to check up on me."

Bull winced. "Ouch."

"And now there's you."

"But I'm not crazy, sweetheart." He took her hand. "Only crazy about you."

"Which is insane"—she yanked her hand from his—"considering you don't me."

"Josephine Belle"—he looked her directly in

the eye — "I'm not going to steal your clothing, or write lewd songs about you, or stalk you."

"What do you call *this*?" She waved between them.

"It's not stalking if you're attracted to me, too."

"That's what I'm talking about," she exclaimed, throwing her hands in the air. "I'm a successful, smart woman. I should be able to find Prince Charming. Not the frog, who's really just a frog."

He *was* Prince Charming. She just needed to realize it. "You don't know it yet, but you've come to the right place, sweetheart. I'm completely sane."

She laughed like it was the funniest thing she'd ever heard.

"What?" he asked, affronted.

"You're not sane. I know crazy, and you're it. Set aside the tattoo and the MBA thing you do — "

"MMA," he corrected. "Mixed martial arts."

"You're a *fighter*?"

"Why do you say it like it's a problem?" He frowned. "I'm good at it."

"You beat people up for a living!"

"Not anymore. I'm making a transition."

She held her hands up. "Okay. Whatever your career choice, as a way of asking me out, you sent me a bustier and asked me to wear it for you."

He waited for the end of the argument, but when it seemed like she wasn't going to finish her statement, he said, "And?"

"That's what I'm talking about!" she exclaimed. "Who *does* that? Only someone who's insane, and I'm not dating crazy anymore." She stood up like she was going to leave.

But he wasn't done. He stood up too and blocked her escape path, careful not to box her in, because she seemed scrappy and not like she'd take well to being pushed around. He liked that, by the way. "There's no way in hell I'm going to let you walk out of my life. Not when I've just found you, and not when you're the perfect woman for me."

She got in his face. "I'm not going to date you."

"Then why did you come here to meet me?"

"To bring back your underwear." She pointed at the box.

"You could have taken it to Nicole, or thrown it out." He grinned, slow and triumphant. "You like me."

"I do *not*," she said with all the prissiness in her body.

"Don't worry, sweetheart." He ran a finger down her cheek to the edge of her lips. "I'll cherish you."

She growled, her fists clenched, and then turned on her heels and marched out.

He revelled in every sway and jiggle as she left. When he turned around he saw the puzzled looks of the patrons around him, and his grin widened. "*That's* a woman," he told the restaurant at large.

Chapter Eleven

JULIE SET A vase of gladiolas on a table in the entrance of the Carrington-Wright mansion, becoming aware of a strange tune as she rearranged the flowers. It took her a moment to realize the noise was coming from her—she was humming.

Humming.

She paused, staring at the tall stems, wondering if she should be annoyed at her sickeningly good humor.

Nope.

She grinned and adjusted the vase one more time. She deserved to feel smug. *Anyone* who got such good loving deserved to be smug. They had another date tonight, and by "date" she meant he was coming over to her place.

Part of her knew she should be concerned about the future. Their lifestyles were nothing alike. But he kept assuring her they'd make it work out, and she was beginning to believe he was right. Hope was a powerful thing.

One place where they were very compatible was in bed. She thought about Scott, naked, over her, under her, and she went simultaneously gooey and edgy. Desire was such a funny thing. The more sex she had, the more she wanted. The more she consumed, the hungrier she was for more.

"You look happy," a feminine voice said from across the hall.

She looked up to find Alexis descending the enormous spiral staircase. Instead of workout gear, the bride had on white pants and a thin orange sweater that hung off one shoulder. "How do you keep those pants pristine?" Julie asked in wonder.

Alexis laughed as she walked into the foyer. "I keep my fiancé away from them. I swear he's like Pigpen."

Scott was just the opposite—always put together. She imagined calling him her fiancé and blushed.

"You're busy at work," Alexis said as she joined her.

Julie studied the bride's expression. "You don't like them at all."

"They aren't my style. It's not your work," she quickly reassured. "It's just that I'm not into fussy things the way Mom is."

"I can see that." Julie frowned, confused. "Why didn't put your foot down? I mean, you seem like a strong, independent woman and not someone who'd bow down to her mother."

"I'm the CEO of my own fitness company. I'm used to being in charge, but then when I'm with my mom it's like I'm five again." Alexis smiled ruefully. "It's okay. Her heart is in the right place."

Julie opened her mouth but promptly shut it.

Alexis laughed. "I know what you're think-ing, but she really does mean well. She wants my brother and me to be happy in our relationships, because she wasn't happy with my dad at all." A cloud passed over her expression. "I loved my dad, but he was an asshole to Mom."

"Where is he now?"

"He died. He had a heart attack in bed with his mistress." She exhaled and then smiled sadly. "So I get why Mom is hands-on in trying to make our lives perfect. It's misguided, but she means well. And it makes her happy, which makes us happy. Between you and me, I really don't care about flowers and parties and colors as long as I get to marry Rob."

"Julie," Elise called from down the hall. "Are you here?"

Alexis gave her a commiserating look. "I

won't say anything if you want to run and hide."

She chuckled. "Your mom isn't that bad, but I don't want to test that."

"Smart woman." Alexis winked at her and strolled off.

Julie shook her head. The bride looked so familiar — she wished she could figure out where she'd seen her before. Still thinking about it, she walked down the hall in search of Elise.

The woman was in one of the front rooms, fussing over the flowers on a table. She looked up as Julie walked in. "Oh, good, there you are. I don't know about this here, Julie. Do you think we can switch it out with the jasmine arrangement that's in the hall?"

The vase of flowers looked perfect where it was. Julie turned to looked at Elise, who also looked flawless except around her eyes, where the skin was pinched with stress.

Normally she'd have just switched the vases

and left it at that—the change wasn't a big deal. But for some reason, instead she said, "I've done a lot of weddings, and anything that can go wrong usually does. Nothing is ever perfect."

Elise looked at her shrewdly. "Are you telling me I'm overreacting?"

"Yes," Julie said frankly. Then she shrugged. "I get it. You want a happy ever after for Alexis. But it's happening, and this is the perfect fairy tale wedding to kick that off."

"You're right." Elise visibly relaxed, even though she shifted the vase one more time. "Thank you, Julie."

Alexis breezed in right then. "Are you torturing Julie, Mom?"

"Of course not. The things you say, Alexis." Elise drew herself up, indignant. And then she focused on her daughter and frowned. "That's not the outfit we bought for today."

"I know. This is actually comfortable." The

bride winked at Julie and then kissed her mom's cheek when the doorbell rang. "I'll get it."

Elise waved a hand as Alexis strode out of the room. "Don't listen to Alexis. I'm not the ogre she makes me out to be."

"Your daughter loves you," Julie said.

"She does, doesn't she?" She smiled softly. "I have lovely children."

"They're lucky, too." Her own mom barely remembered her birthday every year, and her dad always acted like she was intruding the one time a year she visited. She'd never cared, but now that she saw what having a loving mother was like, she felt a pang of regret.

Even if it was crazy to wish for a nagging mother. Shook her head at herself and gathered up the little bit of debris she had left. "I'll just check on—"

Alexis walked into the room, a tall blonde following close behind her. Alexis had a strange expression on her face. "Mom, I believe this is one of your guests."

Elise brightened and walked out hands outstretched. "Zoe, I'm so happy you could make it. Alexis, you know Zoe Blanchard. You were in play school together. Remember?"

Alexis shook her head. "Like when we were three? That was twenty-seven years ago, Mom."

"You must remember each other. You were dear friends."

If Julie had to call it, neither woman looked at each other like they were friends much less acquaintances. The blonde looked like she was on the other end of the spectrum from Alexis. Alexis may have been born into San Francisco's royal family, but she had a down-to-earth quality. Zoe Blanchard looked like a princess: expensive and high maintenance, with her long highlighted hair, manicured nails, and designer outfit. She was an ice princess version of Sophie Martineau.

Elise clasped Zoe's hands and pecked the air around each side of her face. "I'm so happy you came to town for the wedding. I'm looking forward to seeing your parents. It's been an age. Julie, did you meet Zoe? Zoe graduated from Harvard and started a company out on the East Coast, but she's considering returning home."

Julie nodded politely, jealous. Not because of the blonde but because of the glowing way Elise talked about her. Her own mother never talked about her that way.

Elise turned to her daughter, her arm still around the newcomer's waist. "Alexis, take Zoe into the parlor and get her a drink."

Her daughter rolled her eyes, but turned a friendly smile to the blonde. "I don't know about you, but I could use a shot of whiskey."

"Alexis," Elise admonished.

"A double," Alexis amended with a wink. She threaded her arm through Zoe's arm and led her away. "Come on. You can catch me up on what you've been doing with your life since we used to eat grass together."

Julie snorted in amusement, quickly stifling it when Elise frowned at her. "My children don't appreciate how much I love them," the socialite said. She fiddled with one of Julie's perfect arrangements. "But I do love them. It's because of them that I do what I do."

"What you do?" Julie asked absently, resisting the urge to fix what Elise was messing with.

"Zoe. I invited her to be Prescott's date to the wedding." She rubbed her palms against each other. "He won't be happy when he finds out, that's my son's way, but he'll thank me in the end."

Julie was sure that'd be the case. Someone named Prescott Carrington-Wright III had to be a momma's boy.

A door shut loudly somewhere down the hall

and Elise perked up. "Prescott? Is that you, darling?"

Masculine footsteps approached down the hall toward them. Julie tried not to groan—she just wanted to clean up, go home, and take a long bath before her date with Scott. He was coming by later after a family obligation.

She busied herself fixing the flowers that Elise had messed with, hoping they'd just ignore her. She should have known better, though, because as Elise's son walked in, Elise said, "Darling, this is Julie. She's the wonderful florist I hired for the wedding."

"Julie?"

She froze, her head lifted. Elise's son sounded like Scott. She turned around, her mouth falling open as she saw her lover standing in front of her.

Chapter Twelve

JULIE GAPED AT Scott, feeling the gulf between them widen. "*Prescott?*"

"Prescott, darling, you remember Julie, I'm sure," Elise said, oblivious to their shock. "I found her business card on your desk. I figured you've used her in the past."

"Oh, he's used me," she said, hands on her hips.

Scott shook his head. "Julie and I—"

"Haven't actually met," she finished for him, mentally willing him to shut up. She stuck her hand out, eyes narrowed. "Julie Miller. And you're *Prescott Carrington-Wright the Third?*"

He winced. "Technically, I go by Scott Wright."

"I've never understood that," Elise said. "The Carrington-Wrights have been pillars of the community for generations. I don't see why you have to be ashamed of that."

"I'm not, Mom." He kissed her cheek. "I just think it's important to make it on your own merit."

"Hmm." Elise didn't sound convinced, but there was a crash from down the hall that distracted her. "Excuse me. Oh, Scott, come to the parlor. There's someone here you need to meet."

They watched her leave.

And then Julie smacked Scott's arm. "You didn't tell me you're the golden son of the richest family in town."

He rubbed his arm. "Does it matter?"

"Of course it matters. You lied to me."

"I didn't lie," he said firmly. "I go by Scott Wright. I am exactly who you think I am."

"Well, you held out on me, and I'm working for your mom."

"Not forever."

"But I am right now." She gasped, her hands at her cheeks. "What would she say if she found out we were getting it on?"

"She'd say she wanted a family discount on the flowers."

Julie hit him again. "This isn't funny. We have a serious problem here."

"If you think my mom's going to care about who I date—"

"Yes, actually I do." She pointed down the hall. "There's a blonde lurking around who was imported to be your date to the wedding."

He took her outstretched hand. "You're going to be my date to the wedding."

She tried to picture herself at his side while he toasted Alexis and her new husband. Impossible. But she had no trouble picturing Zoe. She tried to pull her hand away. "The help doesn't attend the function."

But he wouldn't let go. "You aren't the help. You're a businesswoman who's providing my mother a service."

"Exactly," she exclaimed. "It's almost like dating my client."

"You don't believe that, Julie." Scott pulled her closer. "What really has you bothered?"

The fact the Elise had brought in Zoe to be Scott's date to the wedding, because even she had to agree Zoe was the better choice. Who'd choose a florist in grubby jeans who hadn't even gone to junior college over a Harvard graduate who looked like a model?

But she knew he'd just deny it, so she gave him something tangible. "It's the competition."

"What does that have to do with us?" he asked, shaking his head in confusion.

"I don't want her judgment affected by my dating you."

He blinked at her incredulously. "You think

she'd *punish* you? She's not like that."

"If I win, I don't want anyone else to think it was because I dated you. That's like nepotism. You said yourself that you wanted success based on your own merit."

"When you win," he corrected.

"*When* I win the competition, I don't want people to have doubts about my ability. I want them to know it was because I rocked, and not because my boyfriend's mom arranged it for me. And you can't tell me people won't think that if they know we're—doing whatever we're doing."

"The only way to avoid that is to not see each other until the competition is over."

"Right," she said, her soul weeping just a little as she retracted her hand.

He crossed his arms. "That's not acceptable."

"It has to be."

She watched the emotions flicker across his expression: disbelief, anger, and finally determination. The determination scared her, and she started to step backwards.

He grabbed her around the waist. "We're not done discussing this."

"Stop," she hissed, looking over his shoulder to make sure no one saw them. "Your mom might walk in on us."

"I really don't care." But he hefted her over his shoulder and walked them into a small room.

Which wasn't actually a room but a large linen closet, she realized after he turned the light switch on. He set her down and then backed her into a corner.

"What are you doing?" she asked suspiciously, retreating until her back hit a shelf. "Are you trying to intimidate me?"

"No, I'm trying to seduce you." He pressed up against her and kissed her.

Logically, there were so many reasons to resist

him, but the moment his lips touched hers, relief flooded over her. She clung to him, wanting to prove she was worthy of him.

Winning the trophy was key. It'd elevate her to an elite status, beyond mere florist. With it, she'd be recognized as an artist.

His hands slid under her shirt, warm on her back. "I'm not going to agree to stop seeing you," he murmured against her lips, "so get that out of your mind."

She really didn't want that either. Somehow, in a matter of days, he'd scaled her walls and wormed his way into her heart.

But she wasn't going to jeopardize her standing in the competition—either way. So she said, "Then we need to keep it on the down-low."

He stilled and looked at her. "Meaning?"

"Nothing in public."

"Define public."

"Like no kissing in the open." She kissed him to demonstrate because he looked perplexed. She nibbled at his lips until he groaned.

He leaned into her, his hardness prominent against her belly.

She reached between them and ran her hand over him. "No groping either," she said, her voice breathy.

If the look in his eyes was any indication, he wanted to eat her up. "What else can't we do in public?"

"No overt affection." She undid his pants and slipped her hand inside his briefs.

He groaned, his head falling back. "Only until the competition is over?"

"Yes." She ran her fingers over him, loving the way he grew harder in her hand.

"And then I can be as affectionate as I want?" he asked in desire-laden voice. He cupped her between her legs, pressed his fingers into her center.

"Whenever and wherever I want?"

Julie moaned. "Hell yes."

"Fine, but for the record, I'm not happy about this."

"Parts of you are happy." She squeezed those parts, just to prove it.

"That part's going to be *very* happy in a moment." In record speed, he unzipped her pants, pushed them off, and turned her around. He nuzzled the nape of her neck and whispered in her ear. "I mean it, Julie. After this is over, I'm shouting it to the world. I won't be a guilty secret."

"Understood." If he still wanted her then. She braced her hands on the shelf in front of her. "What are the chances someone will come find us in here?"

"I locked the door."

"Have I told you how smart you are?"

"Forget telling me. Show me instead. Better yet, promise you'll see me tonight."

She bit her lip, thinking about it. She should

tell him no. She heard him unwrap a condom and looked over her shoulder to see him cover himself.

He stepped up behind her, guiding himself between her legs. "Promise me or I'm holding out."

"You're a bad man." She moaned as he rubbed over a really nice spot.

His other hand held her in front, slipping between, his finger grazing her so she saw bright lights behind her closed eyelids. "I'll come to your apartment around nine tonight, with food," he said as his finger toyed with her.

She gripped the shelf. "Scott—"

"I'll come dressed in all black, wearing a mask, if that's what you want." He pushed in more from behind—slow and torturous—and they both groaned.

"Okay, fine," she said, breaking down.

He thrust into her to the hilt.

She gave in, unable to fight it, telling herself it'd all work out. She'd win the competition, and everything would be fine.

But then he thrust into her again and again — his fingers working her simultaneously — and soon she couldn't think of anything but the feel of him in and around her. She arched back into him, her hips rotating against him, feverishly seeking.

Needing.

Her climax came over her like a tidal wave — shift, strong, and without mercy. She cried out, her head falling forward onto the shelf, not wanting him to stop.

Dimly, she heard him cry out. His teeth bit her shoulder, and with his fingers still gliding over her, the wave crashed over her again, less intense but still potent.

Scott kissed her neck, holding her close and tight. "I'm coming tonight, and so are you, again, over and over. That's a promise, Julie."

She wanted to make some sort of clever quip, but all she could do was nod and hope tonight arrived really quickly.

Chapter Thirteen

BULL LISTENED HALFHEARTEDLY to the woman talking to him, even though it was the chairwoman of Kids in Safety, the main charity he donated most of his time to. He sipped his whiskey, trying to relax. He felt on edge. Normally, a good workout, beating on his workout buddy, a steam, and a smoothie and he was good to go. Lately that didn't work. Lately *nothing* worked.

His life was chaos.

Business negotiations had gone sour. The company who wanted to nationally distribute his smoothie line wanted too much control and too large a cut. He wasn't anyone's bitch — in the octagon or in the boardroom. So after months of going back and forth with them, he finally told them to take a hike.

His dad had commiserated with him, telling him it was just a setback, but Bull wasn't used to not beating his way to a triumphant outcome.

And then there was Josephine Belle. Or, rather, there wasn't, because she wasn't where she should have been—standing there next to him, dolled up and feisty. He'd tried calling at her office to ask her out, but she never took his calls.

Normally, he liked these charity functions. He got to schmooze and be charming and flirt with women in glittery gowns, all while he was doing good. As a famous fighter, he had a duty to use his name and reputation to make a difference. His fans gave him so much—he wanted to give back.

This event was his favorite—not because of the fancy clothes, the gourmet food, or the good booze, but because it was for children. Unlike a lot of charity organizations, Kids in Safety actually put its money where its mouth was. They did a lot of good, hands on, in all sorts of communities, insuring that children grew up with the resources they needed, happy and safe. More than donating his name to the cause, he often worked hands-on with them, going into lower income areas and teaching self-defense techniques, physical and mental, to help the kids stay safe.

Bull listened to the chairwoman of the organization, who was a nice, if chatty woman, as he casually checked out the crowd.

Then he saw her.

Her back was turned, but he'd recognize those sinful curves anywhere. Josephine wore a black, form-fitting dress that ended mid-calf but plunged halfway down her back, revealing her creamy skin. Her hair was piled on her head in some sort of demure twist that contradicted the expanse of skin revealed.

He straightened, suddenly feeling alive. It

took all of his willpower not to stride across the floor and slip his hand into that opening.

Then he noticed the tall man she was speaking to. The dude was leaning toward her.

Bull scowled.

The chairwoman put a hand on his arm. "Is something wrong, Mr. Torres?"

"Yeah, but I'm gonna fix it." He patted her shoulder. "Doing good, Mary. Keep it up."

He turned from her and zeroed in on his woman and the misguided guy who didn't know he was treading dangerous waters.

Bull knew he was also entering dangerous waters, but he couldn't help himself. He walked over to Josephine and put his hand square in the middle of her bared back.

She startled when she felt him, turning wide eyes on him. Her back stiffened under his palm, but at least she didn't hit him or move away.

Hot damn she felt fine against his hand. He

hummed in appreciation. Then he turned to the man and stuck his right hand out. "Hello, I'm Bull."

The man brightened in recognition. "Bull Torres, the fighter. I'm a fan."

He felt Josephine glaring at him. He ran his finger up her spine, satisfied when he felt her shiver.

"You're one of the spokespeople for Kids in Safety, right?" the man said.

Josephine turned to him, stepping away from his touch. "You work with K.I.S.?"

"They do good." Bull shrugged. Normally, he'd be all about talking up the charity, but right now the only thing he wanted was Josephine in his arms. "I promised Josephine I'd take her for a spin on the dance floor."

Josephine glared at him. "No, you —"

He grabbed her hand and pulled her with him. "Don't pout, sweetheart. I know I've been neglecting you, but you know I had a duty to the kids. I'll make up for it."

Josephine let him drag her to the dance floor. He knew she'd be conscious of making a scene and he was using that against her, but nothing stopped her from mentally throwing daggers at his head, and he felt each one.

He pulled her into his arms. "Have I told you I love the way you glare at me?"

"You're insane," she hissed, smoothly following his lead. "What are you doing here really?"

"I told you, I'm working." He pulled her closer. She fit perfectly in his arms. "What are *you* doing here, besides looking gorgeous and distracting me from the spiel I'm supposed to give donors?"

"I donate, too."

He looked at her. "Do you want my spiel?"

"No."

"Can I give you something else?"

"No."

"Maybe later." He dared to touch her back again with the tips of his fingers.

"You do know they're playing a fast song, right?" she asked, trying to wiggle away.

He held her firmly where she was. "I like Timberlake. He's a good guy."

She looked at him dubiously. "You know him?"

"Who do you think gave him the idea to bring sexy back?" Bull smiled down at her, resisting the temptation to kiss her. "You haven't complimented me on my tux."

Her narrowed gaze flickered over his clothing. "It's a change."

"You like it," he said confidently. "You can't compare me to the douches you dated in the past, not while I'm in this tux."

"The douches — I mean, the men I dated before were well dressed," she protested. At his quirked brow, she pouted. "Mostly."

"And you haven't thanked me for saving you

from boring conversation with that man." Bull nodded thoughtfully. "Although he did have sense enough to be a fan, so he wasn't all that bad."

She sputtered, finally exclaiming, "You're impossible."

He moved her in a slow, sexy spin and dipped her backwards, the lovely column of her neck on display. One day, he'd have the honor of kissing her there whenever he wanted. "You have to admit that you find me mildly intriguing."

"Not even," she said, but her voice was huskier.

"You find me more than mildly intriguing." He righted her, tugging her body flush against his. "You have a hard time keeping from throwing yourself in my arms."

"You are so seriously deluded that you're validating my reasons for not going out with you."

"You push me away only because you like me coming after you." He moved his leg between hers. "You're in luck, sweetheart. I know a good thing when I see it. I'm not giving up on you."

"This is ridiculous." She stopped suddenly but didn't step out of his arms. "You need to leave me alone."

"You need to kiss me."

"What will it take for you to go away?"

She didn't say no, and that was enough for him. He lowered his head until the only thing between them was the promise of a kiss. "Go out with me."

She glared at him. "Fine."

He straightened, frowning. "Wait. I thought I just heard you say you'll go out with me."

"Because it's the only way you'll go away."

He wasn't going away, but that wasn't the point here. He held on to her hips so she couldn't escape before they settled this. "You'll go on a date. To dinner or any other activity I choose. With me."

She narrowed her beautiful eyes. "No sexual hijinks."

"Not on our first date." He reared back, like he was affronted. "What sort of man do you think I am?"

She put a hand to her forehead. "You're determined to drive me crazy, aren't you?"

In bed, yes. But he wasn't going to push his luck by saying that. Instead he took her hand from her head and placed the barest of kisses on her knuckles. "Thursday night? I'll pick you up from work."

"I'll meet you there." She looked at him balefully. "What time?"

"Seven, at Gary Danko." He smiled. "Wear something pretty."

She rolled her eyes and pulled away. "Goodbye."

"For now." He watched her walk for a few steps, admiring the sway of her delicious backside. Be still, his heart—and other eager parts of him. "Josephine Belle."

She stopped at the edge of the dance floor and glanced over her shoulder at him. "Yes?"

"If you'd like to wear the underwear I bought you, let me know. I'll courier it to you."

Her gaze narrowed again.

Those sexy cat eyes were going to be the death of him. He wanted to stride up to her and kiss her, but he just smiled and sauntered past her. Women liked butts, and his was particularly excellent, if he said so himself. He sashayed out, letting her get her fill, counting the minutes until he saw her again.

Chapter Fourteen

THE DOOR TO her shop opened. Julie sighed, relieved Sophie had finally arrived. She needed a friend to talk to. Without looking up from the wire she was twisting, she said, "I'm glad you're here."

"That's so sweet," said a chirpy, sweet voice.

Sophie was many things, but she wasn't chirpy *or* sweet. That voice belonged to Dr. Hyacinth Gardner.

Sure enough, Julie looked up to find her nemesis standing in the flower shop, picture perfect in her dress and coat. She scowled. "Did you get lost on the way to your coven meeting?"

"I came to see how you were doing, of course." Hyacinth headed straight for the worktable, her gaze laser-focused on the frame Julie was building. "Is this for the competition?"

She had the urge to throw herself in front of the green foam blocks she was carving, to protect them from the prying eyes. If only she had a big sheet to cover them.

Hyacinth leaned closer, her nose practically pressed against the wire frame. "Is this Sutro Tower?"

"Seriously?" Julie said. Then she realized what she'd done and wanted to smack herself upside her head. Why didn't she just let Hyacinth think that?

"Is it a hill? Twin Peaks?" The woman picked up one of the sketches on the table. "Or maybe it's the start of the seven hills?"

"Give that back." Julie grabbed the paper and gathered up all the other pages. She shoved them inside a basket behind her, well out of Hyacinth's nosy vision. "What are you doing here?"

The woman smiled with all the innocence of the Big Bad Wolf. "I was in the neighborhood and I thought I'd stop by to see how you were doing with your design. Really, Julie, it's time for you to win this year."

Julie's gaze narrowed. "Is that what you think?"

"Well, of course." Hyacinth batted her eyes. "Why bother trying if you aren't going to be serious about it?"

"You're right. I wonder why I didn't realize that," she replied with dripping sarcasm. She kept her fists ruthlessly at her sides even though she wanted to sock Hyacinth.

"The seven hills isn't a bad idea," the woman continued blithely. "However, I wonder if it's 'San Francisco Spirit' enough. Maybe you should do a replica of the Transamerica pyramid in a rainbow profusion of flowers. Or you can build City Hall out of poppies."

Julie crossed her arms. "Gee, Hyacinth, I really appreciate the ideas you're giving me, even though they're what you did in the past."

The woman smiled like a shark and patted her arm. "I just want the competition to be fair. I feel like I have such an advantage, having won it for the past five years in a row. Of course, I do have an edge with my advanced degrees."

She pulled her arm away and looked at the spot where the woman had touched it. Great—now she was going to have to disinfect. "Are you done yet? Because I'm closing up."

"Of course." Hyacinth adjusted her purse on the crook of her arm. "Call me if you need help, okay?"

"Right." Julie glared daggers as her nemesis sashayed out of her store. She was still glaring at the door when it reopened and her best friend stepped inside.

Sophie smiled with her multimillion-dollar smile. "If you greet all customers with that look, it's a wonder you have anyone buying flowers from you."

Julie picked up her clippers and brandished them. "I'm going to kill her. Will you help me hide her body?"

Sophie blinked. "Whose body?"

"*Dr.* Hyacinth Gardner," she said, spitting out each syllable.

"Satan's handmaiden?"

"Yes."

"She was here again?" Sophie asked incredulously. "Doesn't she have the sense to know you're close to going homicidal on her ass?"

"*Close?*" She held up the clippers. "Does this only look close?"

Sophie pushed her hand down. "Don't get me wrong, I'll help you dispose of anyone's body, because that's what friends do, but I'm wearing silk today. Blood doesn't come out of silk too easily."

"You're saying you need a heads up to dress appropriately."

Sophie set her bag down and hopped onto the counter, her normal spot. "You've got to dress for success."

Julie thought about the way *Dr.* Hyacinth Gardner dressed and frowned down at her jeans. "Maybe I don't look like a flower champion."

"What are you talking about?"

"If you have to dress for success, what do I dress like? A homeless person?"

Her friend gaped at her. "Did that woman drug you?"

"I'm just saying maybe I don't look like a winner." She studied the green blocks she was carving. "Maybe it's crazy to think I can win. Hyacinth has a doctorate."

"In what?" Sophie asked, pulling out her notebook and pen. "Being a bitch?"

Julie's lips quirked. "She double majored."

"What's up with you?" Sophie tipped her head and studied her, obviously trying to decipher her. "I've never seen you act anything but secure."

"You've only known me two seconds."

"It's been at least four seconds, and it's been concentrated time. Most couples contemplating marriage haven't spent as much time together as you and I have."

It was true. Aside from being one of the top grossing actors in Hollywood, Sophie was an aspiring screenplay writer and, oddly, did most of her writing in Back to the Fuchsia. She wrote her first script, which was being released in theaters in the winter, sitting on Julie's counter.

But she'd met Sophie after she lost last year's flower competition, and now there was Scott—and the lovely blonde Elise wanted to set him up with. Except Scott kept insisting he wanted to take *her* to the wedding.

Julie shook her head. "I'm just saying she has an advantage on me with her education."

"There's more going on here than you're letting on." Sophie patted the counter. "Want to lie down and tell me all about it?"

"No."

"You know what I think?"

"No, and I don't want to know."

"This is about that man you met."

Julie said nothing. Why had she thought it'd be nice to talk to Sophie? Maybe if she ignored her, Sophie would take the hint and go home.

"I think you like him," her friend said, "and you're intimidated by him."

She wasn't intimidated by Scott, but Zoe and her perfect hair and many degrees unnerved her. "You also think lettuce should be drunk instead of chewed."

"Don't mock my green juices. And don't think

I can't see that you're trying to change the subject."

Julie threw her hands in the air. "Fine. Scott's mom is trying to set him up with another woman to take to the wedding."

Sophie frowned. "And Scott hasn't shot her down?"

"I don't think he takes it seriously. He keeps asking me to the wedding."

"And you're going with him," her friend said as if it were a foregone conclusion.

She frowned.

"Julie, you're going with him to the wedding, aren't you?" When she didn't answer, Sophie exclaimed, "Aren't you dating him?"

"Not really." He'd taken it to heart to keep their relationship clandestine, which made her happy and annoyed her, too—and that annoyed her more, because she never figured herself to be the sort of person who'd ask for one thing and then be disgruntled when she got it.

"Wait"—Sophie held her hand up—"you aren't seeing him?"

"Well, he comes over, yes." She felt herself flush under her friend's quirked brow. "We've been meeting secretly so his mom doesn't find out, so he comes over, hangs out, bugs me about going to the wedding with him, and leaves in the morning."

Her friend shook her head, her mouth gaping. "And he's okay with this arrangement?"

"Not really."

"Tony wouldn't have been either." Sophie studied her. "But you like him."

"His mother imported a blonde to go with him to the wedding." Julie frowned. "I wish I could be angry about that but who can blame her? Elise wants the best for her son, and Zoe is the type of woman you'd expect Scott to end up with."

"It doesn't sound like Scott agrees."

She shrugged. "Zoe's perfect for him. She's gone to Harvard and has an MBA. I never even took classes at a junior college."

"It's not about education. Plenty of successful people never went to college."

"Yes, but when you have billions no one cares. I don't have billions."

"You don't need billions to be successful."

"It must help though, right?"

"I wouldn't know." Sophie looked at her with the candidness that had connected them in the first place. "You're great, Julie. Kind and funny and pretty, even if you don't wear makeup and refuse to dress with any sort of style. If this guy was attracted to you looking like that, he must like you. I doubt he's going to care that you're illiterate."

She rolled her eyes. "Why do I let you come around again?"

"Because you love the attention." Sophie

slipped off the counter. "Seriously, you don't need a college education to win the prince."

"What do I need?" she asked doubtfully.

Sophie smirked like the femme fatale she was. "If I have to tell you that, maybe you *do* need to go back to school, to take an anatomy class."

Chapter Fifteen

*I*T WAS A mad house.

Scott strode down the hallway, narrowly evading a collision with one of the added staff his mother had hired until the wedding. He stifled his annoyance as he changed course and headed to his suite. It was his little sister's wedding—he could be patient until it was over.

If he weren't so frustrated by Julie, it might be easier.

His jaw clenched reflexively, and he rolled his shoulders to ease the tension.

Futile. The only thing that was going to make him happier was seeing Julie. Holding her would be even better. He hadn't seen her since Saturday night, after Alexis's bridal shower. Julie had claimed she was busy with her entry for the competition, but he knew better. She was avoiding him.

He stopped in the middle of the hallway and pulled out his phone to try calling her again. Apparently, he was a masochist.

She answered this time. "What is wrong with you?"

"The woman I'm in"—he caught himself before he said something that'd push her away more—"in*fatuated* with is avoiding me."

"I'm busy," she said indignantly.

"So am I, but I make time for you."

She sighed. "I know," she acquiesced softly. "I'm sorry I'm being bitchy."

"You're being difficult, not bitchy."

"Thanks for clarifying," she said dryly.

"I need you." He had nothing to lose by being

honest and everything to gain. "I'm surrounded by insanity, and it's not helping matters that I miss you so much. If I could just kiss you, I'd be vastly improved."

"I—"

"Here you are, Prescott." His mother rounded the corner, a tall blonde in tow.

"Is that Elise?" Julie asked warily.

He rubbed the back of his neck. "Yes, but don't—"

"I'll talk to you later."

"Ju—"

She hung up.

"Damn it." His finger hovered over the screen, to call her back.

But his mother glided up to him. "What's wrong, darling?"

Everything about this situation. He slipped the phone back into his pocket. "Nothing. I need to go for a run."

"Oh." Her lips pursed, an expression he recognized as disapproving. "I was hoping you'd be here to help Zoe."

He glanced at the blonde. She didn't look like she needed help with anything.

"Where are my manners?" his mom exclaimed in an overly bright voice. "Darling, this is Zoe Blanchard. Zoe, my son Prescott."

He hated being called Prescott for more reasons than one. But he smiled pleasantly and shook the woman's hand. "Pleased to meet you," he lied.

To her credit, she looked amused rather than eager. "Likewise," she said with an ironic tilt to her lips.

She rose a couple notches in his estimation. "You're Alexis's friend?"

"Zoe and Alexis used to go to school together," his mother interjected.

"Play school," Zoe clarified, managing to look serious. "When we were toddlers."

His mom put her arm around the blonde. "Zoe's parents are coming to the wedding, and when I found out Zoe was in town this week, I told her she just had to come over to be part of the festivities."

He arched his brow at the woman. "How fortunate for you."

She bit her lip, obviously trying not to laugh. "I was thinking that myself."

"Zoe's having lunch with us today. I thought afterward you could take her around to see the neighborhood," Elise said not subtly at all. "She's thinking of moving here from Boston."

"It's too bad you're going for a run," Zoe said with insincere remorse. "Maybe another time."

He could have hugged her, he was so grateful for the out. "Sure. Mom has your number, right?"

"Of course I do, darling." His mother frowned at him. "But I'm sure you can go out for a run anytime."

At that moment, KT rounded the corner from

the back of the house and stopped abruptly at the end of the hall. "Oh crap," she said audibly.

Scott turned to his mom with a smile, improvising quickly. "I wish I could cancel my run, but I promised KT I'd go with her."

"You did?" his friend asked warily.

"Yes," he said firmly. "You want to get into shape, remember? You hate the little pooch to your belly."

She put a hand on her flat stomach. "Um. Yeah. I'm a slob."

He smiled at Zoe as he backed up. "It was nice meeting you. I'm sure we'll run into each other."

She nodded, smiling. "No doubt."

"Prescott—"

"See you later, Mom," he said over her, turning to stride toward his friend. KT gave him her patented stink-eye, but he ignored it and took her arm. He whispered to her, "You owe me for all the times I've hidden you from *your* mom."

"Truth." She sighed, trudging along next to him. "Do I really have to run though? I'm allergic to exercise."

"How about a brisk walk around the block?"

She sighed. "Don't say I never did anything for you."

"Come to my room so I can change shoes."

"Are you still using that line?" She asked, following him into his room and flopping on his bed. "It was old by the time you got to fourth grade."

He pulled out his phone and tried calling Julie back, but her phone went directly to voicemail. "Damn it."

"What's got your Jockeys in bunch?" KT asked. She watched him, her head half dangling from the edge of the bed.

"My dating life is complicated." He went into his walk-in closet, changed into workout clothes, and grabbed his tennis shoes.

"Aw man." KT frowned at the shoes in his

hand. "You were serious about the brisk walk, weren't you?"

"I know you prefer climbing hedges, but this'll good for you." He raised his brow at her as he laced one. "Consider yourself lucky that I'm not insisting you run with me."

She heaved a sigh. "Damn your complicated dating life."

He grinned. "That's the spirit."

She got off the bed and stretched her back. "The chick downstairs isn't the one you're dating, is she?"

"Why?"

"Because I've always hated Barbie dolls. They're creepy," she explained as they headed outside. "If you hooked up with her permanently, I might be tempted to chop off her hair and twist a limb off."

"Then it's good for Zoe that I'm not interested in her. She seems like a nice person though."

"Do you want 'nice?'"

"No, I want Julie."

Snorting, KT saluted her accomplice Celeste as she opened the kitchen door that led outside. "So Julie's not nice, huh?" she asked when they were on the sidewalk.

"No. She's a lot like you." He grinned at the indignant look she shot him. "To tell you the truth, she is like you in that she's a straight-shooter. She's honest and tells it like it is, the way you do."

"Then she must be a great catch."

"Or supremely strange," he said with a straight face.

"To*may*to, to*mah*to." KT gestured with her hand. "So are you going to tell me what the problem is, or do I have to sit on you and drag it out?"

"She won't go out with me publicly."

"Finally!" She threw her arms in the air. "A woman of discerning taste. What did she say? She can't be seen with such a preppy guy?"

"She's a florist, and she's entering some competition that my mother chairs, and she doesn't want my association with her to color anyone's opinion of her entry." He frowned. "The thing is I can't blame her. If I were in her shoes, I'd want to ensure the same thing. I *do* the same thing."

"So the problem is...?" KT huffed as they headed up a hill towards the Presidio.

"She won't see me at all." It pained him to say it. "In other words, I miss her."

"You know what I love?" she asked, breathing heavily. "That there's a woman in the world who isn't falling all over herself to become Mrs. Prescott Carrington-Wright III. She must be awesome. I can't wait to meet her."

"You make me sound pompous."

KT arched her brow but didn't say anything.

"I'm not pompous. My name is, but I'm fairly grounded."

"At least as grounded as a millionaire playboy can be."

"Billionaire," he corrected with a grin.

"I rest my case." She paused at the edge of the Presidio, just under the Arguello gate. "This is where I stop."

"You don't want to play basketball with me at the YMCA?" he teased.

"Hell no." She jerked her thumb over her shoulder. "I'm catching a cab back home. And by 'back home,' I really mean to your place."

"I guess your mom is still pressing you about men?"

"*Pressing?*" KT gaped at him. "She's crushing me with these demands to date. The thing is she can't possibly understand what it's like to be the daughter of Anson and Lara. It's like I'm a rock princess, and they all want me for the person they think I am."

He nodded. He understood perfectly. It was why he'd unofficially shortened his name to Scott Wright.

His friend gave him a baleful look. "It's *so* far removed from who I actually am."

He knocked her shoulder gently. "You'll find someone who'll love you for yourself and not your family."

"Like Julie loves you?"

Julie hadn't told him she loved him—yet. If she insisted otherwise... Well, he'd deal with that when the time came. "I'm going to marry her, KT."

KT tipped her head and studied him. Then she nodded and patted his flat stomach. "Then you better go get into shape. No woman's going to want a slob."

"Careful or I'll give Lara a map to your hiding place." He grinned when she cheerfully flipped him off as she strolled back toward their homes.

Chapter Sixteen

BULL STOOD OUTSIDE Gary Danko, propped to the left of the entrance. He knew he must look like he had all the time in the world, leaning against the wall with his hands in his pockets, but he watched the street vigilantly, waiting not-so-patiently for Josephine to arrive. The valet attendants must have picked up on his vibe, because they gave him a wide berth.

He checked his watch. Two minutes until.

Part of him was annoyed that she wouldn't let him pick her up, but most of him loved that she was playing hard to get. It brought out the predator in him.

He knew he was a brute, but he was roughness covered in silk. Any woman who took him on needed to acknowledge that and appreciate it. Except he didn't want just any woman—he wanted Josephine Belle.

A taxi slowed down on the opposite corner. Bull pushed off the wall, alert, knowing instinctively that it had to be her.

Sure enough, she stepped out from the other side of the cab. The taxi took off, and she turned and met his gaze.

He exhaled, tension draining in a rush. He didn't give her a way to cancel the date—she didn't want him to have her phone number, so he didn't offer his. And he didn't think she'd stand him up, but it'd been a possibility.

If she had stood him up, he'd have been crushed.

He took her in. Instead of her usual sexy librarian look, she looked like an uptight spinster from Eastern Europe. She wore all black, her skirt hitting halfway down her calves. She had on a gray coat that covered all of her up. She even wore mannish black-rimmed glasses.

He grinned, not taken by the ruse. *Game on.*

She walked toward him, her nose in the air. Her clunky black shoes made a dull sound on the pavement. "Good evening," she said in her sweet Southern voice, pushing her glasses up her nose.

"Yo," he said deliberately, just to see her cute nose wrinkle. He resisted the urge to laugh as he leaned in to place a peck on her cheek.

Damn, she smelled good. He brushed his nose against her skin, inhaling her, before putting distance between them. "Love the look," he said enthusiastically.

Her brow furrowed. "You do?"

He nodded with a straight face. "The only thing that could make it better is if you covered your hair with a scarf."

She stared at him. He knew she was trying to figure out if he was serious or not. He smiled, liking that he had her off-balance. Taking her elbow, he escorted her toward the restaurant.

"You aren't really taking me to Gary Danko, are you?" she asked suspiciously.

"I am." He nodded to the valet who held the door open for them. "It's one of my favorite restaurants in the city."

She didn't look convinced.

He grinned. He was so going to enjoy this.

The hostess, Gretchen, smiled wide when she saw him. "Mr. Torres! It's a pleasure to see you again. I hope you've been well."

"Thank you, honey." He gave her a hug. "How's that boyfriend of yours treating you?"

She brightened. "He's my fiancé now."

"Smart man. Congrats." He kissed her cheek, loving the way she beamed.

"There's a couple seats at the bar. Want to take

them, or would you like a table tonight?" Gretchen glanced inquisitively at Josephine.

Bull smiled proudly, putting his arms around his woman's waist. "The bar would be great."

"This way." She walked them to the seats at the far end, secluded from the rest of the bar. Gretchen pulled out the chair next to the wall for Josephine, discreetly winking at him.

His smile turned into a grin. At the bar, he'd be closer to her than sitting across from her at a table, and putting Josephine in the corner created an air of intimacy. He'd have to send the hostess a bottle of champagne to enjoy with her fiancé.

Gretchen demurely wished them an enjoyable dinner and left them.

Josephine speared him with a confused look. "You come here often."

She stated it, but he knew it was a question. He smiled at her and held out the menu. "They have great scallops. Want a cocktail?"

She frowned, absently taking the menu. She looked him up and down, her frown deepening. "This is one of the best restaurants in the city."

"I like the best," he said mildly as he opened the menu.

"But you look like you're at home. You even dressed..."

"Yes?" He could feel her staring at him, but he kept his gaze on the menu. Let her have the opportunity to check him out, because he knew he looked good tonight. He wore slacks, a patterned shirt open at the collar, and a dark velvet jacket. He hoped at some point she'd want to run her hands on the soft fabric.

"Nice," she said finally.

He smiled pleasantly at her. "Thanks."

Her brow furrowed even more, as if nothing made sense.

"Let's get you a cocktail, sweetheart. That'll help." He patted her knee and waved the bartender over. "Juan Carlos, my friend would like a French 75, and I'd like some Thunder Chicken. But not the classless Thunder Chicken. The high-end stuff."

"Thunder Chicken?" Josephine repeated, seemingly despite herself.

Juan Carlos nodded. "A French 75 for the lady and Wild Turkey Rare Breed for you, Bull. Neat?"

"Please." He leaned toward Josephine, partly because he knew it'd throw her off and partly because he loved the fruity smell of her hair, clean and soft in contrast to her severe look tonight. "What are you thinking of having for dinner?"

She set the menu aside and speared him with a flat look. "I have questions."

"About the menu?" he said innocently, even though he knew that wasn't what she meant.

"About you."

"I'm an open book, sweetheart." He held his arms out. "Read me."

Her gaze narrowed. "How many times have you been married?"

He smiled, loving the game she was playing. "None."

"How many children do you have?"

"Ten." He laughed at the way she gaped. "Just kidding. I don't have any."

"Are you sure?"

"Sweetheart, I'm a successful fighter. If I gave them a chance, women would crawl out of the woodwork, claiming to be pregnant with my babies. So, yeah, I'm careful."

"You don't want children?" she asked, her brow furrowing.

"I want to have children with the right woman, if she wants to have them." He dipped his head closer to her. "Our babies would look beautiful, don't you think?"

She got that haughty look that turned him on so much. "That's rather presumptuous."

"Just asking for what I want." He nodded in thanks as Juan Carlos set their drinks in front of them. He held up his glass to Josephine Belle. "To us."

Her eyes narrowed, but she was too polite to turn down the toast. She sipped delicately at her cocktail. He took a swig of his whiskey, sighing as it warmed him all the way down. At her questioning look, he explained, "It's like a punch to the face with a velvet glove."

Her cute nose lifted in the air. "Well, then, since you're a fighter you must love that."

"I told you, I'm transitioning out of fighting."

"To what? Pornography?"

He chose to be amused rather than offended, because he knew it'd irk her more. "Think I'd make a good porn star? A sweet Southern lady like you shouldn't be having such thoughts, should you?"

She glared at him and lowered her gaze to the menu.

He set his chin on his fist and grinned at her. He *loved* when she got prissy. "Do you have more questions, or can we order food?"

"Did you graduate from high school?" she asked instantly.

"Yes." He didn't think she needed to hear that he'd graduated from Stanford, as a business major.

"How many times have you been arrested?"

"For felony crimes or minor misdemeanors, like nudity?" He grinned at her schoolmarm glare, doubly entertaining with the glasses she wore. "Never, but I'd be happy to let you cuff me."

Juan Carlos interrupted them with a polite cough. "Are you eating with us tonight?"

"Yes," Bull said, "and we're ready to order."

Before Josephine could say anything, he ordered the five-course dinner for them to share, selecting a range of luscious food he thought she'd enjoy.

When the server disappeared, Josephine rounded on him. "What if I were vegan or vegetarian?"

"Are you?"

"No."

"Then it's not an issue." He took a sip of his whiskey. "But it'd have been your fault."

Her eyes narrowed. "How?"

"You won't tell me anything about you. If I make a mistake, it's because you're withholding information from me."

"This date isn't about me."

"I know. It's about proving that I'm *not* worthy." He sat back. "Want to try with some more questions?"

"How many women have you given that corset to?"

"One," he said honestly. Before she could get indignant, he said, "You."

Her lips puckered as though she'd tasted

something sour, but her eyes reflected confusion.

He handed her drink over. "Have some, sweetheart, and then you can tell me when you'll put the corset on for me."

She took a large sip.

"My mom always told me I drove her to drink, too." He smiled fondly. "My folks are coming out to visit me next month. You'll love them. My mom is tiny but fierce, and my dad is a big teddy bear. Are your parents still around?"

"Yes." She hesitated, but then she must have decided to relent and be a little more pleasant because she added, "They live in Georgia."

"That where you grew up?"

She nodded. "I've been in San Francisco a couple years."

"Isn't it strange that a Southern girl specializes in Asian art?"

She touched her hair, pulling at a spot as if it were too tight. "My grandmama had a kimono that my granddaddy brought back from Japan in World War II, and the pattern on it enchanted me."

He pictured her in a silky red kimono, his corset peeking from underneath. *Down, boy.* He took another sip of whiskey, trying to calm himself. "Love at first sight?"

"Something like that."

"So you believe in love at first sight?"

Her gaze narrowed. "Don't push your luck."

Not a yes, but not a no either. He'd take that.

Their first course came out, split on two plates, which bummed him out a little. He'd had visions of feeding her from a shared plate.

"What are you going to be doing if you're no longer fighting?" Josephine asked as she forked a ladylike bite into her mouth.

"I'm selling smoothies." He knew she'd assumed he was opening a smoothie stand on the corner instead of looking for national distribution, but he figured she had to get over underestimating him on her own. "You don't know it, but I make killer smoothies."

She gave him a flat look. "Smoothies?"

"It's gonna make me a fortune," he said brightly. He knew exactly what she was thinking: that he was a fool. But she was about to get a rude awakening.

Over their next courses, he launched into a discourse on branding, market share, and projected sales that would have bored a venture capitalist. He talked about production schedules and deliverables, press releases and advertising copy. He threw in buzzwords left and right, loving the way she looked more and more confused the longer he talked—not because she didn't understand the lingo but because she couldn't comprehend that *he* did.

By the time their cheese course arrived, he figured he'd given her enough food for thought. "But that's enough talk about work. Let's discuss us."

"Us?" she repeated carefully.

"Obviously you think don't think I measure up, so why don't you tell me why or how so we can deal with this head on. You think I'm like the men in your past because...?"

The confusion in her expression multiplied. He saw the doubts, that the past hour of business 101 he'd sprung on her was not the conversation she'd expected them to have.

She wiped her mouth with her napkin and set it aside. "You're a fighter."

"I was. I'm retiring." An awful thought occurred to him, and he scowled. "You don't think I'd hurt you, do you?"

"Of course not," she said quickly, not sounding convincing.

"That's bullshit," he exclaimed, not caring that other people were staring. He leaned closer to her, getting in her face so there'd be no question of his seriousness. "I protect those I love. I'm going to cherish you, Josephine Belle. I can't guarantee I won't be a knucklehead at times, but I'd never purposefully hurt you. Especially physically. I can't believe you'd even think that."

"I'm sorry," she said softly.

He glared at her, still hurt. "I'm going to tell Nicole on you."

"Fair enough." She shook her head, looking as though she'd fallen through a rabbit hole. Then she said, "Is that the time?"

He glanced at the wall clock. It was almost eleven. "Are you going to turn into a pumpkin?"

"Yes. I have an early meeting."

He signalled the server for the check, making sure it was expedited and to get them out the door quickly.

Outside, she looked at him, wary.

Good—she deserved it. Let her be off-balance, the same way he'd been ever since he laid eyes on her at the fashion show.

Hell, he was done being a nice guy. Forget not pushing — he was going on a full-court press. Before she could say anything, he kissed her the way he'd been imagining for days, like the world was ending.

She gasped. She didn't put her arms around him, but she didn't pull away either. He undid her clip and ran his fingers through her tumbled hair. Better. Soft. He fisted it gently and brought her closer. The frustration and hurt of the evening dissipated into warmth and a longing so deep it felt rooted in him.

When he released her, she had a soft look on her face, the flush of pleasure. She'd have that look on her face when they made love.

He couldn't wait.

He signalled the valet, who instantly had a taxi stopped with the door opened. Josephine licked her lips, her eyes still passion dazed as he escorted her to her ride and waited for her to get inside.

Before he closed the door, she leaned over with a slight frown marring her beautiful face. "I still won't wear your corset."

She would—even she knew it. But he just smiled like a hopeful fool as the cab whisked his woman away.

Chapter Seventeen

JULIE DROVE AROUND Laurel Heights, looking for a spot to park the flower truck. Usually she didn't have trouble, but it made sense that today she would. Today was the day from hell.

Three things had happened: Hyacinth had stopped by the shop *again*; Julie lost her entry form for the competition; and she was late to deliver a large order and had to eat the charge to appease the customer.

Julie yanked the parking brake, growling as she got out of the car.

It'd all worked out. She kicked Hyacinth out, created a new application for the competition, and made her customer happy. But it'd left a bad taste in her mouth.

Especially the missing competition entry packet.

She'd had it all ready to fax that morning, only when she'd gone to do it, the packet was gone.

How could it be gone? Yes, Hyacinth had been snooping again, but she shouldn't have been able to find it. Although the woman *did* have a pact with the devil. Julie wouldn't put anything past her.

In the end, she'd gotten her packet faxed to City Hall in time.

She gripped the steering wheel and focused on parking. The spot she found was an inconvenient four blocks from the shop, but right now she'd take what she could get.

When she turned the corner, she saw a person standing in front of her store. She tensed—was Hyacinth back?

But it wasn't a woman. It was a man.

Scott.

Her steps slowed as her heart sped up. She felt a flash of happiness seeing him, and then she remembered the perfect blonde his mom had shipped in to be his date for the wedding.

He straightened when he saw her. Hands in his pockets, he looked casual, but she could see the tension around his shoulders and jaw. He watched her warily, like he didn't want to scare her off.

"This is very public," she pointed as she pulled out her keys.

"I'm here to buy flowers." He took the keys from her hand and unlocked the door.

"No, you aren't."

"No, I'm here to kiss you, but as far as anyone else is concerned, I have a need for daisies." He motioned her inside. "I may also try to convince you to be my date to my sister's wedding."

She sighed and dragged herself inside. "It's already been a long day, and I don't have it in me to fight you."

"Then don't fight." He stood in front of her and cupped her face. "Just go with me, Julie. It'll make both of us happy."

She wavered, torn, wanting to say yes. The wedding was the day after the competition, so she wouldn't be on the line for that any longer.

But what if she lost again? She'd had to half-ass her new drawing to get it in on time today—what if the judges didn't like it? What if Elise found her San Francisco Spirit idea ludicrous? Julie wouldn't be able to bear being at the wedding, knowing that every time Scott's mom looked at her she saw a failure.

That thought hurt. She'd never admit it, but lately she'd been imagining Elise was her mother-in-law. Without the trophy, Elise would have no reason to show her off—not the way she could with Zoe.

So she shook her head. "I can't go with you."

He sighed. "I think we can work this out to a mutually beneficial end."

"The only beneficial end for me is to win the flower competition."

"Maybe it's not about winning." He tipped her head up and kissed her.

It was gentle but she still felt it all the way to her toes. She ruthlessly stifled the hum it generated in her belly, stepping back to put distance between the two of them. "I need to win."

"Okay, you need to win. I understand that." He crossed his arms. "But do you need to push away the man you're going to spend the rest of your life with in the process?"

She put her hands on her hips. "That's kind of arrogant, isn't it, Prescott?"

He grabbed her by the waist and pulled her into him. "It's the truth, Julie, and you know it. Stop playing difficult."

"I'm being realistic, not difficult." She looked him in the eye. "I need to prove I can win, on my own merit, not because I'm dating you."

He dropped his forehead against hers. "I admire your drive to earn this on your own, but don't shut me out. I miss you, Julie. Don't tell me you don't think about me."

She thought about him all the time. Her mind should have been consumed with the competition but it was full of him and wondering if he was hanging out with the blonde Elise wanted him to date.

But before she could voice any of that, he kissed her.

All thought left her mind.

He caught her ponytail in his hand. "Let's go to your place tonight. We'll order dinner in and hang out. No pressure, no public places."

She hesitated, really wanting to say yes. "I can't."

He moved away from her. "I knew you'd say that, but I'd hoped you wouldn't. Bye, Julie."

"That's it?" she blurted, unable to help herself. "You're just leaving?"

"What can I do?" he asked with sincere curiosity. "You keep pushing me away. I can't even get you to agree to be my date for my sister's wedding, and that's after your competition."

"Wouldn't you rather see if I won first?" she said as jokingly as she could. "You wouldn't want to be seen with a loser."

"I want to be seen with *you*, Julie. A trophy isn't going to change how I feel about you."

But it would change how she felt about herself.

Scott shook his head. "If you change your mind, call me."

"Or?" she asked hesitantly, afraid of the answer.

"There is no *or*." He shoved his hands in his

pockets. "Either you want me or you don't. It's easy."

Only it wasn't. She watched him stride out of the shop, fighting the panicky feeling that she'd screwed up beyond repair. She almost rushed after him, to drag him back into her arms, but she imagined the prestige she'd gain from winning and told herself it was better this way. Just until after Friday.

Chapter Eighteen

BULL PACED IN his kitchen, trying not to crush the phone in his hand.

He really wanted to though. He was *this* close to storming downtown to the Asian Art Museum and laying siege on Josephine's office. He'd been trying to get a hold of her since the night of their date. Was it too much to ask for, to call to say he had a great time?

But he didn't have her cell number, so he had to call her at work. And the gatekeeper who guarded her wouldn't let him through. It was probably on Josephine's orders, but that didn't improve matters any. He'd been on hold for five minutes.

He hated being on hold.

His doorbell rang, so he walked through his house to answer it. Usually, every time he strolled through his pad, he appreciated it. Sleek modern wasn't everyone's thing, but he loved it. It was big and shiny, just like him.

Today, though, it just looked empty and cold, like it was lacking. The thing it was lacking was Josephine's beautiful presence.

He opened the door to Ethan's happy face. It made him scowl. He gestured Ethan in as the dragon lady came back on the line.

"I'm sorry. Josephine isn't available right now. May I take a message?" she said in a pseudo-polite voice that conveyed her annoyance.

Damn it. He rubbed a hand over his head as he followed Ethan back to the kitchen. "When will she be free?"

"Her schedule is completely booked for the rest of the day."

"So she's not eating lunch? Or taking a break?"

"Is there a message I can give her or not?" the woman said, her voice losing the veneer of false cheer.

"Yes. Tell her to expect a package in the mail." He hung up and threw the phone across the room.

"Lady troubles?" Ethan asked, pulling out a stool at the counter.

He nodded. "I need a drink. Wheatgrass?"

Ethan grinned. "I'm not sure I can handle the hard stuff so early in the day."

"Bite me." He glared at his best friend as he went through the process of snipping the wheatgrass he grew in the window and juicing it. Pouring it into two shot glasses, he slid it across the counter to Ethan. "It's a double."

Ethan chuckled and then downed his shot like it was tequila. "Want to tell me what has you worked up?"

He set his hands on the counter and leaned forward. "Josephine Belle Williams."

Ethan's eyebrows shot up. "She sounds like a handful."

Bull pictured her lush curves and growled in need.

"I guess she is." Ethan smiled. "She's making your life difficult, I assume."

"The woman is damn infuriating." He began to pace again. "She won't date me because she thinks I'm crazy."

Ethan nodded. "Obviously she's astute."

"I'm the most sane person we know."

"Yeah, but look at who we know. MMA fighters aren't the most stable people in the world. We *choose* to get the shit beaten out of us for a living."

Bull crossed his arms. "I win my matches."

"You still get beaten up."

"Which is why I've decided to retire."

"Retire?" Ethan set his shot glass down and focused on him with all the intensity he used to give his opponents in the octagon. "Since when did you decide to retire?"

"Since last year." He sighed and pulled out a stool to perch on. "I'm getting old by sports standards."

"You're smart. You're getting out intact, on your own terms." Ethan had been forced to retire early because of a head injury, but he had come to terms with it once he met Valentine, who showed him there was more to life than wishing for things that would never exist. "What are you going to do instead?"

He liked how Ethan knew him well enough to realize he could sit idle. "I want to take my smoothies national."

"That's fantastic." His buddy clapped him on the shoulder. "Are you opening chain stores or distributing to outlets?"

That was the thing about Ethan: he was a businessman, too. Bull took a deep breath and, on the exhale, got everything off his chest—the frustration of being so close to closing a deal and having it fall through and the uncertainty of finding another backer.

Ethan listened patiently, arms folded, leaning against the counter. At the end of Bull's venting, he said, "So your frustration over Josephine is compounded with the ambiguity of your business. You know what you need?"

"Besides a few million and good loving from my woman?"

"Yeah, besides that." Ethan's lips quirked. "You need to make progress on one front. Either make a contact that could help with capital for your smoothie line or contact Josephine."

He slumped, pouting. "She won't take my calls."

"What package are you sending to her?"

"I bought a corset a year ago from Nicole."

"You've known Josephine that long?"

"No, I just met her, but I was prepping to meet her."

Shaking his head, Ethan grinned. "You *are* crazy, man. But knowing you, it also makes sense."

"The corset is her size. I know it. But she thinks it's insane and won't try it on."

"I'm sure you'll find a way to convince Cinderella to put it on."

Bull nodded. "I just have to show her I'm her Prince Charming."

"That's going to take a lot of convincing," Ethan said in a deadpan voice.

He gave his friend a look. "Did I harass you when you were wooing Valentine?"

"Yes." Ethan grinned. "I'm just returning the favor. Have you talked to Nicole about the guy who invested in her lingerie line? He might not be a good fit, but he's in that business. He'll have contacts."

"That's brilliant." Bull perked up. "See? I always told people you were more than a pretty face."

Shaking his head, his buddy pushed off the counter. "Let me know how it goes."

"Better still"—Bull stood, putting a hand on his friend's shoulder as they walked out—"I'll invite you to the launch party for my smoothies and to my wedding, whichever happens first."

Chapter Nineteen

JULIE DRAGGED HER feet about going to the Carrington-Wright mansion to set up for the rehearsal dinner until she was bordering on being late. Scott would be there.

In the car, driving over, she winced, thinking about their last encounter. She hadn't seen him since. He hadn't stopped by at night or even called, and she didn't know where they stood.

She didn't know where she wanted them to stand. The last time she saw him had left her raw and confused. She was afraid she wouldn't be able to resist him.

Well, she knew she couldn't resist him. Scott was some serious catnip to her.

Four blocks away, her phone rang. She answered, murmuring a vague greeting as she concentrated on making it through the intersection.

An unfamiliar voice asked, "Is this Julie Miller, of Back to the Fuchsia?"

"Yes."

"This is Leslie Nelson. I'm the coordinator for the San Francisco Flower Competition."

Julie sat up, instantly alert. They'd never called her before. "Yes. How can I help you?"

"I received your application and plans for your design."

"I'm really excited about it," she said, heart beating.

"It's a really great design, but unfortunately someone has already submitted something very similar, so we're going to have to ask you to resubmit a different idea."

Julie hit the brakes hard as she got to a stop sign. "*What?*"

"The deadline for entering has passed, but since you'd made the deadline I checked with the chair and got an okay to give you an extension, so it's all good as long as you come to the competition with the packet including your entry form and design sketch."

"It's not all good!" she protested. "How can someone else be doing the same design?"

The missing drawing and application.

She had a sinking suspicion in her gut. Swallowing thickly, she asked, "Is it Hyacinth Gardner?"

Leslie paused for so long Julie didn't think she was going to reply, but then the woman said, "I can't reveal that information."

Telling enough with that pause. Julie put a hand to her head. "Okay, this isn't your fault. Thank you for giving me another chance to enter."

"Off the record," Leslie said in a lowered voice, "I wouldn't put anything past Dr. Gardner. I'm sorry this happened."

Julie murmured something incoherent and dropped the phone next to her. Now what was she going to do? The competition was next week. It'd taken her a couple months to come up with the idea, and another couple weeks to build the foundation for her sculpture. She had less than two days to come up with not only a winning design but the physical product.

She was screwed.

A driver behind her laid down on his horn. Julie flipped him off out the window but tore through the intersection, pissed.

Beyond pissed. Crushed, too, because that design was the best thing she'd ever done. Now she wasn't sure how she was going to top that—in a week.

Since she'd been over so often, Elise had given

her a code to get in the gate. She buzzed herself in and drove around the back. She got out of the Element, her hands shaking.

She took a deep breath. She'd deal with it—one thing at a time. For now she needed to focus on getting the rooms decorated for the rehearsal dinner.

One of the maids helped her unload and carry everything inside. Most of the arrangements were already made, but she held off assembling a couple centerpieces so that they'd look less staged and more organic to their setting. She instructed the maid where to put the vases, and then turned her attention to the flowers in front of her.

"Oh, excuse me."

She turned around to find a woman in the doorway. She recognized her instantly as Zoe, the woman Elise had set up for Scott.

"I think I'm lost." The woman smiled in self-deprecating humor. "I was looking for the living room, but I'm turned around somehow."

"It's just down the hall." Julie pointed to the right.

"Thank you." The blonde started to walk away and then stopped. "You're the florist, right?"

"Yes." Julie stiffened. This was the part where they always told her how to do her job better.

The blonde smiled brightly. "Your arrangements are beautiful. I'm not much of a flower person, but I notice yours. Very beautiful and not typical. Do you have a card? I'm going to give it to my mother, who spends a small fortune every week on flowers. Why should the other florist get the business when you're so much better?"

Frowning, Julie took one from her pocket.

"Thank you." The woman beamed and strutted out.

Julie stared after her. And then she banged her fist on the table. Wasn't it enough that she was tall, golden, and gorgeous? Wouldn't you know it that she was also nice?

Annoying.

The worst part of it was that she could see Scott with her, and the picture was heartbreakingly perfect. That blonde was the type of woman Prescott Carrington-Wright III should spend his life with, not someone like Julie.

The thought was *very* depressing.

As she packed up, she imagined herself with Scott. She could see it, but the picture was fuzzy. She couldn't see where they lived — not this mansion and certainly not her studio — and she couldn't see traveling with Scott all over the world.

But she could picture daily life, with Scott telling her about his day as they sat on the floor, naked, eating takeout, and it was great.

She sighed, and then she cursed. Damn it — she forgot her favourite clippers inside. Remembering exactly where she'd left them, she hurried back in to grab them.

Sure enough, they were on the table in the dining room. She picked them up and headed back out.

Scott's laugh echoed down the hall. Julie paused, a pang of longing overcoming her. Without thought, she moved toward it.

A woman's voice sounded, followed by more of his laughter. Julie stopped, frowning, knowing she should turn around and leave. Only her feet had a mind of their own and kept walking toward the parlor, as Elise called it.

She peeked in the room, seeing Scott and Zoe together. Zoe had her hand on his arm, her other hand gesturing with great animation. Whatever she was telling him was apparently funny, because Scott was laughing like there was no tomorrow.

They looked so perfect together, like they were a photo right out of *Vogue*, advertising the way everyone wanted their relationship to look.

How could Scott want to be with her when he

had Zoe in front of him? Not like he seemed to remember that she existed right at this moment.

That pissed her off. But she was more pissed at herself for letting herself believe that she could have him. The trophy was out of reach, and so was Scott. She'd been a fool to think differently.

She stormed down the hall. If only this week were over. Then she could go back to normal and just do flowers. She was good at that. She didn't need to be more.

"Julie!"

Scott's voice caused her to stiffen, but she didn't stop.

"Julie, wait."

She walked faster, hearing him jog after her.

Unfortunately, he caught her arm right as she got to the door. "Let me go," she said tightly.

He frowned at her. "You're upset. What happened?"

"Seriously?" An incredulous puff of laughter

escaped from her lips. "Maybe you and Zoe can talk about it and figure it out."

"Zoe?" The confusion on his face turned into dawning comprehension. "Nothing's going on between me and Zoe. We were just commiserating over being set up with each other for the wedding."

"Uh-huh." She tugged her arm. "I need to go."

"I'm serious, Julie." He stepped closer. "I'm still holding out hope you'll be my date."

"Don't hold your breath." At his hurt expression, she sighed. "Look, it's just best if we don't see each other."

He dropped her arms. "Best for who?"

"Everyone." She steeled herself. "We don't belong together. It's so obvious. Just because the sex is good—"

"Good?"

"Okay, great," she acquiesced. "But great sex doesn't mean we belong together forever. I think we're making a mistake."

"You're saying this is a mistake." He yanked her toward him and kissed her.

She melted against him despite herself. She wanted to grab him closer and hold him forever, just like this, because she loved him.

She loved him.

But then they broke apart and she noticed his really nice shirt under her hands, and his watch, and the shine of his shoes. The intelligence in his eyes. She had worn jeans on, and her fingernails were ratty.

He deserved so much more. She pulled away, her heart breaking.

Scott folded his arms and studied her, his expression stern. "So this is it? You're giving up?"

She frowned. "I'm not giving up."

"Then what do you call this?"

"Reality."

"Your reality is screwed up." He turned and walked away, anger in each step.

Julie wilted against the door. Her brain told her she'd done the right thing, but her heart told her she was an idiot.

Elise walked into the hallway as Scott rushed by her. The smile for her son faded into a confused frown as she looked at Julie. "What's going on here?" she asked, walking toward her.

Julie wanted to let her know that her son was an ass, but she had a sneaking suspicion that the real ass here was herself.

"Julie?" Elise reached out to her.

She shook her head, swallowing the tears that she refused to let loose, and hurried out of the mansion, where she didn't belong anyway.

Chapter Twenty

"I'VE GOT A bone to pick with you, Carrington-Wright." Megan Steiner strode into his office and shut the door behind her. She faced him, hands on her hips, looking like a vengeful Valkyrie with her fur-topped high-heeled boots and fuzzy poncho. Megan defied every stereotype of what people expected a top venture capitalist to look like. "What the hell is wrong with you?"

"This is a first." He arched his brow and leaned back in his chair. "Usually you like to tell *me* what's wrong with me."

"Yeah, well you're throwing me for a loop, so I'm returning the favor." She sat in a chair across from him, crossed her legs, and swung her booted foot.

To say he and Megan had a contentious relationship would be a lie. If he had to define their relationship, he'd call it sibling-esque. She was like the older sister he never wanted, who enjoyed torturing him a little too much.

"I'm waiting." She tapped the chair's arm, as if he needed audible evidence of her impatience.

What had him off his game was Julie, but like hell was he going to tell Megan he was lovesick. "Want to tell me what this is in reference to?"

"Seriously? This is how you're going to play it? You're *really* in bad shape if you can't think of a better way to evade my inquisition." She rolled her eyes. "Fine. The Spotted Cow acquisition."

He nodded. "I admit I dropped the ball on that one."

She pointed at him. "I saved your ass. You're welcome."

It wasn't critical, but she had saved the firm several hundred thousand dollars. He liked to think he'd have caught the mistake he'd made—eventually—but it was fortuitous that Megan had noticed it before it was an issue. "I appreciate it."

His coworker gaped at him, her lipsticked lips comically wide. "Okay, now I know something is wrong. Did you have an accident I don't know about? Get a concussion?"

He smiled ruefully. Falling in love was an awful lot like being hit over the head, actually. "I'm just dealing with some personal things."

"I knew it." She threw her hands in the air. "This reeks of woman. I can practically smell her perfume all over you."

"Julie doesn't wear perfume."

"Julie?" Megan's nose wrinkled. "Is she a stripper?"

"*Julie?*" He laughed. "No, she's a florist. What makes you think Julie is a stripper name?"

She shrugged. "You just seem like you'd go for that type."

He arched his brow. "Thanks."

"Any time." She got up.

"That's it?" he asked, surprised. "No words of wisdom? No cautionary tales?"

"You want words of wisdom about relationships from *me*?" She shook her head. "Now I know you're bad. I haven't had a relationship with anything other than my vibrator in who knows how long."

"Thanks for sharing that with me," he said with an amused smile. "That's just what I need to know about a colleague."

"I'm a woman. I've got needs." She shrugged. "I'm not going to pretend to be sexless."

"Would it be sexual harassment to say I'm surprised you don't have a boy toy on the side?"

"Yes." She grinned. "But I like that you think I *could* have a boy toy."

Megan was stunning by any standards — not as beautiful as Julie, but attractive in her own way.

And she was successful. "You could have anyone you want."

"That's the thing. There's no one I want." She smiled self-deprecatingly. "So if you've found someone you want, don't screw it up. It's one in a million, finding someone you want to spend time with."

"And if she doesn't feel that way?"

"There's a woman who doesn't want Prescott Carrington-Wright III?" She pretended to be shocked. Then she resumed her regular jaded expression. "Convince her. Enlist her friends. Women always listen to their friends, it's baffling, but people find you charming."

"You're really great for my self-esteem."

"Someone has to keep you straight." She tossed her hair over her shoulder and strutted out of his office.

He stared after her. She had a point about enlisting Julie's friends. He didn't know any of them, but he knew who'd have a clue about her friends: Nicole.

He grabbed his coat and left work. Julie may be willing to give up, but he wouldn't. Ever.

It was after normal work hours, but Nicole didn't do normal. She'd probably still be at her workshop. He drove with a purpose, getting across town in record time. He parked the car in the building's garage, jogged up the stairs to her studio, and knocked on the door.

To his surprise, a big bald man opened the door. He didn't look friendly, even though he had the pale outline of a flower on the side of his face. "If you're selling something, we aren't buying," the mammoth said.

"No, Bull." Nicole hurried from across the room. "That's Scott, my investor. Remember? I told you about him."

"Oh yeah. Just the man I wanted to see." The

man's expression changed from looking like he wanted to pound him to being impressed. "You've got good taste, dude, investing in our girl here. Come on in."

He held out his hand. "Scott Wright."

"Bull Torres."

Scott studied him. "The fighter?"

"Yeah, though I'd rather be a lover." The big man sighed unhappily.

"Excuse him." Nicole gave Scott a welcoming hug. "The woman he wants is giving him fits."

"I belong to the same club," Scott confessed. "That's why I came here."

Nicole groaned. "I only deal in romance. If you want relationship help, you should download my friend Valentine's matchmaking app."

"Actually, I came to ask how well you know Julie Miller."

"Julie, from Back to the Fuchsia?" Nicole

shook her head. "I know her in passing. Grif buys flowers from her. I've seen her with Sophie Martineau though. I think they're close."

"The actress?" Scott had a hard time believing that. Sophie Martineau oozed glamour. One of the things he loved about Julie was that she didn't even bother to put on lip gloss.

"Yeah." Nicole shrugged. "But I hooked up with a rock star, so go figure."

But he knew Nicole and Griffin Chase had known each other for a long time, before he was a rock star. Maybe Julie and Sophie were the same way. "You wouldn't happen to know how to get a hold of Sophie?"

"Sorry." Nicole shook her head. "Can't help you there, but I see her around the neighborhood. I think she lives in Laurel Heights part-time."

"You're attacking from the sides," Bull said suddenly, looking at him with increased respect. "Smart. If only I knew who had Josephine's confidence."

Nicole turned to Scott. "Bull isn't very lucky in love at the moment, either."

"Or in business." He faced Scott, his gaze shrewd. "I wouldn't mind going over some ideas with you, if you're up for it. No strings, man."

"I'd be happy to try to help." Scott clapped his hand on the big man's shoulder. "Over a drink?"

Bull gaze narrowed. "You drink wine?"

"Whiskey would be my choice."

"I knew you looked trustworthy. Let's rock." Bull nodded and kissed Nicole's cheek. "Later, kid. Thanks for nothing."

"I told you I can't give out more information on her." Nicole walked them to the door. "But I provided you a drinking partner. That's got to count for something."

Scott winked at her as he and Bull walked out. "We'll make it count. Thanks, Nicole."

Scott and Bull only had two drinks each, but in that time they'd talked about hardheaded women and the smoothie business. They'd also come up with solutions for all three problems: Julie, Josephine, and Bull's stalled business.

He asked Bull for a prospectus for the smoothie line. It wasn't up his alley, but it was definitely up Megan's. A man learned a lot about someone's character sipping whiskey, and what Scott had learned impressed him. Bull was a man of action, and he'd decided to take action with the woman he loved. Scott wasn't sure he agreed that the action Bull wanted to take was prudent, but if anyone was going to pull off that plan, it was the fighter.

Scott came up with a plan to get Julie back, he was going to track down Sophie Martineau and appeal to her to help him win Julie over. He'd already sent a text to a friend who was in entertainment, to get Sophie's contact info.

Not in the mood to deal with anyone, he took

care not to make noise as he let himself into the house. Surprisingly though, even with the imminent wedding and a house full of people, but there wasn't a peep downstairs. It was late—everyone had probably gone to bed.

Relieved, he jogged up the stairs, and was almost to the third floor when he heard, "Prescott darling?"

Stifling a curse, he turned around and headed back to the second floor landing. His mother stood at the bannister, looking up at him, her brow pinched. "Why aren't you asleep, Mom?"

She lifted her face for a kiss on the cheek. "I'm a little wound up about Saturday. I thought I'd raid your bar for the sherry I like."

He rubbed her back reassuringly. "The wedding is going to be beautiful. Alexis and Rob are going to have a happy life together."

"They will, won't they? It's all I've ever wanted, for the two of you, for you to be happy."

"I know," he said softly. He wanted the same for her, but she never listened when he brought it up. She'd given up on herself a long time ago, putting her energy into them instead.

"Which brings me to you." Her gaze hardened. "What's going on between you and Julie?"

He crossed his arms. "Nothing you need to concern yourself with."

She crossed her arms, too. "When my florist, who I quite like, storms out of my house in tears, I think I have a right to concern myself."

He winced, hating the idea of Julie in tears. He couldn't contact her to see if she was okay—she wasn't taking his calls. He'd even gone to her apartment once, but she hadn't answered the buzzer.

His mom put a hand on his arm. "Are you dating each other?"

"We were."

"What did you do?"

He smiled ruefully. "Thanks for your faith in me, Mom."

"It's nothing personal, darling." She squeezed his arm. "Men are just clueless at times."

"Truthfully, she entered some flower competition that you're judging and she didn't want her entry to be judged unfairly one way or another."

His mom blinked, her hand at her throat. "Does she think I'd score her poorly because she was dating you?"

"I don't know what she thinks. She won't tell me. She's more than a little annoyed by Zoe's presence, too."

Elise had the grace to wince. "That may have been poorly planned on my part. However, in my defense, I had good intentions."

"Is this the part where I can point that you shouldn't meddle in other people's lives?"

"Of course not, darling. I'm your mother. Your birth certificate grants me to right to meddle in your life." She touched his arm and tentatively asked, "Do you love her?"

"She's going to be my wife."

Gasping, she covered her mouth with her fingers.

He pointed at her. "And you'll be accepting of her."

"Of course I will be." She looked completely affronted. "I *like* her."

"Good." He studied his mother, who'd started thinking, which made him very nervous. "What are you plotting, Mother?" he asked warily.

"Nothing." She waved her hand. "It's just that I won't be able to bully her about the flowers for your wedding. Julie will have definite ideas, and I'll have to respect them. Oh well."

He smiled. "I like how you're making the best of a less-than-ideal situation."

"I try, darling." She patted his arm. "Don't worry. I'll talk to her before Alexis's wedding."

"You will not." He put every ounce of forceful-ness he had into the command. "*I'll* work this out, Mom. Stay out of it."

"You're right. Before the wedding isn't the time." She nodded absently, squeezing his arm be-fore heading back to her room.

"Weren't you going to get some sherry?" he called after her.

She smiled over her shoulder. "I'm much bet-ter now, knowing that you've found love. Good night, darling."

He wished he could feel the same. "Good night, Mom."

Chapter Twenty-one

"MOMMY, WHY IS that man wearing a red bow? Can I have one?"

Bull winked at the little girl, who was the only person bold enough to ask why he was sitting on a bench in the Asian Art Museum with a floppy ribbon tied around his neck.

The girl's mother looked at him askance as she said, "We'll get you a bow when we go home."

He nodded to them as they passed, drumming his fingers on his leg. The bench wasn't comfortable, and the bow was strangling him, but he was determined to do this. He was determined to show

Josephine Belle once and for all that she should give him a chance.

It turned out that when a man showed up at the museum wearing a tuxedo and a ribbon tied around his neck, the information desk wasn't enthusiastic about escorting him to their curators. But there had been one kindly woman who pointed out the secure door behind which Josephine's office supposedly lay.

Now he just had to wait. His favorite thing.

He made a face.

Talking to the venture capitalist that Scott worked with had been infinitely easier. He'd had a meeting with Megan Steiner that morning, and she was awesome. She was knowledgeable about food lines and distribution. She needed to look over his prospectus, but he had a good feeling about it. His gut feelings were never wrong.

Which is why Josephine Belle's resistance chapped his hide. He *knew* they'd be good together. If only he could convince her to give them a chance.

The inconspicuous door opened, and Josephine stalked toward him, her heels clacking with purpose. Her eyes were narrowed, and her face was flushed with probably anger, though he liked to think some of it was pleasure at seeing him.

Adrenalin shot through his system, just like before a fight. Picking up the package next to him, he stood up, ready to state his case. "Before you say anything," he began when she stopped in front of him, "I think you should hear me out."

"You're making a scene," she said, her voice a low hiss.

"No, I'm just here to give the woman I want a gift. Me." He showed the package in his hand. "Since the corset wasn't doing it for you, I thought maybe I might."

Her eyes narrowed.

"Before you say anything, I'd like to state that

if you were serious about not liking me, you'd have sent guards to escort me off the property." He pointed a finger in her face. "You wanted to see me. You can't deny it."

She grabbed his finger and pushed it out of her face, but she didn't let it go. "I did not want to see you."

"Your delicious lips say one thing and your eyes say another." He stepped toward her. "Come on, Josephine Belle. You know you want to unwrap me."

For a moment she looked like she was going to give in and say yes, but then her stubborn chin lifted and she shook her head. "You won't get me to play along with your craziness."

"Okay." He nodded, pretending to be way more nonchalant than he was feeling. On the inside, he was seething with frustration. "I admit it. I'm crazy. I'm crazy about *you*, Josephine Belle. I want to laugh with you, cry with you, hold your hair when you're puking, and generally annoy you for the rest of your life, because I have no delusions about that. You're going to get annoyed with me sometimes, just like you are now."

He stepped up to her, touching her face. "But I want to love you for the rest of your life, too. I want to give you presents like this corset. I want to give you kisses and the best loving you've ever had. I want to learn every inch of that gorgeous body of yours, until I know it blind. I want to listen to your dreams and encourage you to go for them. I want to tell you my dreams and know that you'll have my back, too.

"I want to worship you, Josephine Belle. You may think I'm crazy, but I'm only just crazy about you. If you don't get that, *you're* the crazy one."

She blinked at him, her mouth gaping. In her eyes, there was a glimmer of hope.

He felt an echo of it in himself. He took a step closer to her, willing her to reach out and take the corset—willing her to give them a chance.

But then something that looked an awful lot like fear shuttered her gaze, and she shook her head. "You're mad. No one does this."

"No one is us, and I'm only mad about you." Hurt, feeling like a two-hundred pound weight had crashed on his chest, he smiled bitterly. "But I get it. You don't want this."

"I—" She stammered, shaking her head.

"No worries, babe." He stepped back, tossing the corset down between them.

She opened her mouth a couple times like she was searching for what to say. Finally, she gestured to the package. "Don't leave that here."

"Why the hell not?" He shrugged. "I bought it for you. If you don't want it, what do I need it for?"

"Another woman," she said, as if it were such an obvious answer.

Okay, *now* he was pissed. He pointed at her, trying to keep his cool but knowing he was one step away from grabbing her and kissing her into submission. Not that it would work, but it'd be a lot of fun. "If you think I'd give that to just anyone, *you* are the crazy one. I've only ever wanted you. From the moment I saw you, I knew you were the woman for me. You're smart, you're feisty, and you're hot. At least I used to think you were smart. Now I'm having doubts."

Her eyes narrowed. "Excuse me?"

"Don't go all prissy on me, like you're offended. You heard me. I've laid myself all out for you. I've promised you loyalty and love forever, and you've done nothing but toss it back in my face. I'm starting to think you aren't as smart as I thought. And, you know what? Maybe I don't want to date crazy either."

Her back stiffened visibly. "*What?*"

"You're obviously bat shit if you're turning

down the best man who's ever turned up in your life." He leaned, in her face. "And you know what, Josephine Belle? I think you know that. I think you know what you're giving up here, but you're too scared to take a chance. And that's the craziest shit of all. You're going to throw away the best thing that's ever happened to you because you're a little afraid that it may be too good to be real."

Shaking his head, he turned around, for the first time seeing all the people gathered around them staring.

Whatever—let them stare. He held his arms out. "She gave all this up, to be safe. Well, now she can stay in her ivory tower all by herself."

As he strode down the hallway, he heard one woman say "I'd totally unwrap him."

Old Bull would have stopped and let her. Current Bull only felt the pain of his heart being stomped on by a librarian-looking woman in heels.

Chapter Twenty-two

IT WAS HOPELESS. Julie slumped on a stool at the worktable, staring disconsolately at the drawings in front of her. She had no idea how to depict "San Francisco Spirit." It was hard to capture spirit when you didn't feel any at all.

She closed her eyes, trying to regroup. In the dark of her mind, she'd expected to see Hyacinth's saccharine smile as she accepted the trophy for the sixth year in a row. Instead she saw Scott's disappointed expression as she told him to go to the wedding with Zoe.

She put her hands on her head. What had she done? The thought of him even looking at another woman twisted a knife in her chest, much worse than anything Hyacinth could do to her.

Except that she couldn't call him to ask him not to go with Zoe. The thing was, he deserved someone great and accomplished—a match to himself. The last thing he needed was a florist who couldn't even guard herself from being sabotaged.

So even though the competition was tomorrow and she had no clue what she would do, her thoughts were all on Saturday and the wedding.

She hoped with all her heart that she'd have the flowers done and be gone without seeing Scott with the other woman on his arm.

The door to the flower shop opened. Her head jerked up. She thought she'd locked it, because she didn't have it in her to deal with customers today.

Sophie frowned into the dark store from the doorway. "Julie?"

"Go away."

Instead, she flipped the light switch on.

Julie covered her eyes. "What the hell?"

"I knew it," her friend said.

She pried one eye open, still bothered by the lights. "What?"

"You screwed up with the guy." Sophie sauntered over and set her bag on the counter. "And now you're wallowing."

"I'm not wallowing. I don't wallow."

Setting her bag down, Sophie lifted her brow.

Julie crossed her arms and tried not to pout too overtly.

Sophie perched on the table and brushed Julie's hair back from her face. "Want to tell me about it?"

"No." She bit her lip to keep it from quivering.

The door opened again, and they both looked up.

Elise Carrington-Wright strode in, looking like the queen coming to collect heads.

Julie held her hand up. "You have nothing to worry about. I'm not seeing Scott any longer."

"I didn't take you for an imbecile." Elise frowned as she marched toward her. "I hope this is an aberration and not a trait you'll pass on to my grandchildren."

Grinning, Sophie held her hand out. "You are someone I must meet. Sophie Martineau."

Elise accepted the hand regally. "The actress, yes. And a friend of Julie's?"

"Julie is the best woman I know"—Sophie speared the older woman with a narrowed look—"and I won't let anyone hurt her."

"Even herself?" Elise asked.

"Even then." Sophie tipped her head. "And you?"

"I've come to take myself out of the equation." Elise turned to Julie. "I realize I shouldn't have pushed Zoe on Prescott once he made it clear that he wasn't interested in her, however I choose to look at it as a brilliant move on my part."

"Brilliant?" Julie blinked incredulously.

"I'm sure having her here pushed Scott closer to you, and I refuse to believe otherwise. But that's neither here nor there." She lifted her chin. "I don't know what transpired between you and my son, but I can assure you that I won't stand in your way. To be honest, I'm a little disappointed that you thought I'd object to begin with. I don't know why I gave that impression. I liked and respected you to begin with, but I feel doubly so given Prescott's feelings for you."

"What feelings?" Sophie asked.

Julie poked her friend in the ribs.

"Stop that." Sophie pushed her away and returned her attention to Elise. "What feelings?"

"Prescott intends to marry her." The socialite's expression softened. "Love is all I've ever wanted for my children. My parents had it. My father used to tell me the story of how the first time he saw my mother he knew she was the one. He walked right up to her, introduced himself, and then kissed her until her toes curled."

Julie swallowed, remembering that night at Grounds for Thought. Scott had done exactly that. "And they had a happy life?"

"The best," Elise said with feeling. "I foolishly chose status instead, and I was never happy. I won't have that for Prescott and Alexis. So whatever you think will happen with the flower competition—"

"It doesn't matter anymore," Julie interrupted. "I'm out of the competition."

"What?" both the other women exclaimed. Sophie added, "Have you been sniffing the hydrangeas again?"

She rolled her eyes. "Do you even know what hydrangeas are?"

"No." Her friend shrugged. "It was the first flower that came to mind. But that doesn't matter.

What happened with the competition? You were going to kick that Gardner woman's ass."

"I think she stole my design, though I won't know for sure until tomorrow. Not like it matters, because I can't come up with anything as good to represent San Francisco Spirit." She waved at the papers in front of her.

Elise strode to the table and picked up a few sheets, her brow furrowing. "These aren't bad."

"But they aren't good either. Definitely not good enough to win."

The older woman set the pages down. "Have you considered doing something with the Giants?"

"The Giants baseball team?"

"The Giants pull the city together in a way that nothing else does," Elise said. "When they win the World Series, the entire city celebrates. They represent the city's diversity and determination, and they inspire loyalty. They bring everyone in San Francisco together as a community."

"Community," she repeated, sitting up straighter. Then she looked at the socialite. "What made you think of the Giants?"

"I'm quite a fan." Elise resettled her purse in the crook of her elbow. "I have season tickets. My father used to take me, and it was one of the few things I didn't lose when I married into the Carrington-Wrights."

"And yet you're encouraging me to marry into the family," she pointed out.

"Yes, but my son is exceptional." She winked.

Julie let the idea roll around in her head, a design already forming. But she shook her head. "I can do the design, but it took me weeks to shape the foundation for my panorama, much less adding the flowers. And I have the wedding flowers to finish, too."

Sophie grabbed her purse. "I can help with that. I'll be right back."

"Where are you going?" Julie called after her.

"To round up the troops." She pointed at Elise.

"I'm assuming you're going to stay and help?"

"I wouldn't have it any other way." The older woman set her purse down and took off her jacket as Sophie hurried out of the store.

"What's going on?" Julie asked, confused.

"Community." Elise smiled. "We're going to help you finish your competition entry."

What? Surprise made her blink, and emotion clogged her throat. She swallowed a few times before she could say, "You're a judge. Is that allowed?"

"I'm known for my meddling," Elise said proudly. She pulled a stool closer to Julie's and sat primly on it. "And while you draw a plan for our creation, I'm going to tell you how I'm meddling in your affair with Scott."

Julie gaped at the woman. "I can't decide if I'm in awe of you or terrified."

"My children say the same to me all the time." Elise smiled happily. "You're going to fit into our family just fine, Julie."

Chapter Twenty-three

IT COVERED A whole table, a brilliant array of roses, chrysanthemums, and orchids. Dyed straw-flowers dotted the undulating edge of the entire panorama, representing the people of San Francisco. In the center, in preserved orange gladiolas, was the Giants' logo, with the Bay Bridge in the background and a sea of iris for the bay.

It looked amazing.

Julie hugged herself. It was more than amazing, not because of her design but because of the love and support that had been poured into making it. Love and support for *her*.

Sophie put her arm around Julie's shoulders.

"I've got a flask strapped to my thigh, if you need a swig."

She smiled faintly, watching the judges walk up to her display. "I'm okay for the moment, but I may change my mind."

"Just let me know." Sophie adjusted the dark glasses she wore. "I don't know how you're handling this so calmly. I'm a blithering mess on the inside, worse than I was at the screening of my first movie."

Julie put her hand over Sophie's. "It's logical that you'd be nervous. You made this happen."

"I just rallied the masses."

Sophie did more than rally the masses. Sophie brought back half the neighborhood to help set up and decorate the panorama and help with the floral arrangements for Alexis's wedding. The women she'd coerced into coming to Back to the Fuchsia were amazing. Julie knew them from the local stores, and some of them, like Eve from Grounds for Thoughts, bought flowers from her. But she'd never taken the time to get to know them.

Talk about being an idiot. They were amazing. She shook her head, thinking of the way they'd cheerfully flooded into her shop and helped out. And they weren't idle women. Eve ran a busy coffeehouse and bookstore, Olivia had her lingerie store, Lola left her own deadline. Nicole had her lingerie line, her friend Valentine was also a successful businesswoman, and their other friend Marley chronicled it all by taking pictures in between prepping flowers. Gwen, an artist herself, had been especially valuable, directing everyone when Julie was occupied elsewhere.

She felt like she had a whole crowd of new best friends. If she were ever going to conquer the world, she'd call all those ladies together to help. She shook her head, abnormally overcome with emotion. "I don't know how to thank everyone, and especially you."

"We don't need thanks. We did it because we believe in you." Sophie squeezed her. "And we women of Laurel Heights stick together. If we got closer, do you think we'll be able to hear what the judges are saying?"

"I don't think I want to know." She watched the five officials confer in a small circle. Elise was one of them.

Elise had been the most surprising of all. She'd been there the entire time, helping. She even called Alexis to come. Julie felt bad making the bride help with her own arrangements and bouquets, but Alexis had joyfully said it was much better than what was going on at their house.

The judges wrote things down on their score-cards and moved on to the next display. Elise glanced at her and winked.

Julie let out the breath she was holding. She'd made the woman promise she wouldn't judge her panorama with a bias, since she'd worked on it.

Elise had waved aside her concerns, saying that if she didn't think her future daughter-in-law was fabulously talented, she wouldn't have been there in the first place.

Future daughter-in-law.

That wasn't guaranteed, not with the way she'd left Scott hanging. Elise had told her that he'd made it abundantly clear that Zoe was a pleasant woman but not for him. Elise had also been determined to fix the situation. She had a plan.

Julie shuddered, thinking about it. It could go horribly wrong—or very right.

The thing was, if she won, would Scott know that her decision to be with him had everything to do with him and nothing to do with winning the competition? She still wanted to win, just to see the look on Hyacinth's face. But yesterday, surrounded by an army of Laurel Heights women, she'd realized she didn't need a trophy to prove herself. Proof of how awesome she was had been all around her—she'd just been blind.

Sophie leaned down to whisper, "That woman is so smug."

She knew instinctively who her friend talked about. Her gaze swung to Hyacinth's table, where she stood smiling happily, a copy of the panorama Julie had originally designed in front of her.

"Normally, I'd be beyond pissed," Julie said in a soft voice, "but for some reason I just feel sorry for her."

"That's because your display is better." Sophie lowered her glasses and looked menacingly at the woman. "Would it be frowned upon if I went and sat on hers?"

Julie laughed softly. "I'd pay you to do that."

"I was waiting for the right moment to tell you, but I did a little research on our friend Hyacinth."

Julie faced Sophie, who looked very self-satisfied. "What?"

"Let's just say if my name was Bertha Jansen, I'd change it, too." Sophie lowered her voice.

"Bertha only has an AA from a community college in Northern California, by the way."

"The poor woman," Julie whispered, shaking her head.

"Seriously?" Her friend put her hands on her hips, frowning. "That's all you've got to say about her? After everything she's done?"

"I'm going to win. That's all I wanted." Not true, because she wanted Scott more. She frowned at the display from a newcomer on the other side of the room. "Did you stop by the Sunshine Flower panorama? It's her first year here."

Sophie nodded. "It was great for a first year effort, but not as great as yours, or even the one you designed that Bertha stole."

She faced her friend. "I think Sunshine Flowers should win."

Sophie shook her head, confused. "Wait, I think I just heard you hint that you're thinking of giving the win to someone else."

"You heard right." Julie looked at the young woman. "I talked to her earlier. Her business is struggling. The PR a win would bring her could be the difference between making it or breaking."

"You pretend to be an ogre, but you're really a marshmallow on the inside." Sophie hugged her. "Don't worry. I won't tell anyone your secret."

"I better go tell Elise I'm withdrawing."

Sophie pushed her toward the judges.

Head high, she marched over to them. "Excuse me."

They all turned to look at her, but Elise was the first to respond. She smiled fondly at her. "Yes, darling?"

"I'm withdrawing from the competition."

The judges stirred, looking perplexed and disturbed. Once again, Elise was the one who spoke. "You really don't want to do that, Julie. Trust me."

She was going to win—she heard the undertone. She smiled, happy, even more confident this was the right choice. "No, I really do want to withdraw. There's someone who deserves to know he came in first, not a trophy."

"He?" one of the other judges said, scratching his head.

"This is rather unorthodox," another muttered. "Will we have to recalculate the scores?"

"Of course not, Hiram," Elise said. "The next runner up was—"

"Sunshine Flowers?" Julie offered helpfully.

Elise didn't miss a beat. "Yes, it was, the Sunshine Flowers display shows marvellous talent for one so young and untried. We all thought so, didn't we?"

There was a murmur of consent. Julie thanked them quietly and returned to Sophie.

"Well?" her friend asked.

"It's all worked out."

"You're amazing. Insane, but amazing."

The judges conferred again and then one of

them went to the podium that was set up in front of the room. Everyone hushed as he tapped the microphone.

"Thank you all for coming today and being part of the twelfth annual San Francisco Flower Competition. This year, we've had an unprecedented number of excellent entries." He paused as people applauded politely, lifting the trophy off its pedestal. "Unfortunately, there can only be one winner. It gives me great pleasure to announce this year's recipient of the golden Gerbera—"

"Golden Gerbera?" Sophie covered her mouth to stifle her laugh, but her eyes gave her away.

"*Shh.*" Julie elbowed her ribs. "It's coveted."

"—so without further ado"—the judge made a sweeping gesture—"Amy Bendel of Sunshine Flowers!"

Shocked applause broke out. Julie looked at the young woman, smiling at the stunned look on Amy's face as she practically skipped up to receive her prize. Yes, she'd made the right decision.

Next to her, Sophie gasped. "Oh no, she isn't."

Julie became aware of the murmur traveling through the room. She looked where everyone seemed to be focused, and noticed Hyacinth — or Bertha — sauntering up to the podium.

There was stunned silence as Bertha reached for the trophy, her phony smile in full force.

"Dr. Gardner," the judge whispered, not aware the microphone was still amplifying him. He tugged at the trophy as she pulled. "You didn't win this year."

"What?" Hyacinth blinked. Then she looked around the room, her cheeks staining beet red as everyone gawked at her. Then she saw Amy, standing on the other side of the podium. Horror widened her eyes, and she quickly stammered, "I know I didn't win. I thought as reigning champion I'd hand the trophy to Amy. Here you go, Amy."

"Nice save," Sophie muttered as everyone

clapped in disjointed disbelief. They watched Amy go up to the podium and pry the trophy out of Hyacinth's gripping claws.

As the new winner gave a stammering acceptance speech, Elise wound her way through the crowd to join them. She put her arm around Julie's waist, on the opposite side from Sophie, and whispered in her ear, "You're the clear winner, darling, in so many ways."

She had to swallow a couple times to dislodge the lump in her throat. "I hope Scott thinks that."

"He does. Just remember that he thought that before the rest of us did."

"Except me," Sophie chimed in.

Julie grinned. Then she laughed, because it was so much better than curling up in a bundle of nerves.

Chapter Twenty-four

MEGAN STEINER PERCHED on the stool and crossed her arms. "Okay, I'm ready to be turned on."

Bull rubbed his hands together. He'd been looking forward to this morning for the past twenty-four hours, ever since Megan called and said she wanted to arrange a smoothie tasting for her and a potential investor. "You want to get it on without the other dude? Should we wait?"

"I like threesomes as much as the next girl, but if I have some advanced product knowledge I can move the conversation forward in a mutually beneficial way." She pushed one of the shot glasses he'd lined up. "So hit me, baby."

He poured three different shots: what he considered his basic smoothie, and two speciality juice blends. He watched like a hawk as Megan tasted each one, making notes.

He liked Megan. He could tell she was sharp from the first moment he met her, not to mention that she asked the right questions. He had a good feeling about their synergy, and for the first time in days he felt hopeful about at least one thing in his life. It almost made him not care that the personal aspects were in the shitter.

Almost, and only when he'd had enough whiskey.

The doorbell rang.

"About time," Megan muttered as she wrote down some notes.

"I'll let him in." Bull hopped off the barstool and straightened his shirt as he walked to the front door. He didn't bother to hold back his happy grin as he opened the door.

But it faded fast when he saw that, standing on his stoop, in addition to Megan's colleague Smelly James, there was Josephine Belle Williams.

Bull wished that he could have been impervious to her charms, but even standing there in her coat, with her hair up and that vaguely unapproving schoolteacher expression he wanted her. Badly.

Smelly smiled and grabbed Bull's hand, pumping it vigorously. "Smelly James. And you're, of course, Bull Torres. I saw you in Vegas a couple years ago. I put down ten thousand on your fight, and you made me a happy man that night."

Josephine looked back and forth between them, the space between her eyebrows scrunched, which was *not* a good sign.

Smelly glanced at her and then leaned toward Bull, whispering in a way that the entire neighborhood heard him. "Does she want you, too? Because I am *very* interested. Megan spoke highly of you."

"Megan?" Josephine said, her brow lifting.

He grinned. His woman was here, and she was jealous. Both good signs, right? He laughed out loud and waved both of them in. "Come in and we'll get this sorted out."

As he closed the door, Megan yelled from the kitchen, "You're never going to get lucky if you're always late, Smelly James. I've already had a taste and I can tell you what you're missing out on."

"Maybe I shouldn't be here," Josephine said, stopping in the middle of the hall.

"Yes, you should," Bull said as Smelly said, "No, because Bull is mine."

Before she could think he was part of some freaky three-way, he said, "Smelly and another investor are here to check out my smoothies. They might invest."

"Knowing what I do of you and your endeavors, I'd say it's highly likely," Smelly said. He pointed down the hall. "The kitchen is this way?"

"Yeah. Megan's already there." He waited

until Smelly was out of hearing before turning to Josephine. "How did you know where I live?"

"Nicole gave me your address."

"So it's okay for her to give my address to you, but I'm not safe?" He rolled his eyes. "Thank goodness double-standards are dead."

"It's not Nicole's fault." Josephine shifted the weight from one leg to the other. "This is obviously not a good time, so maybe I should—"

"*No.*" He grabbed her hands to keep her from going anywhere. "This shouldn't take long. Why don't you sit in, and then we can talk? I still don't understand why you came."

"I really don't either." She pulled her coat collar closer to her neck.

"But you're here."

She looked him in the eyes. "Yes."

He exhaled and then nodded. "Good. Okay."

She put her hand on his arm. "You probably shouldn't keep them waiting."

"No." He took her hand—he couldn't help himself—and they joined Megan and Smelly in the kitchen.

Megan looked up, curious, as they walked in. "Who's this?" she asked with all the forthrightness he gave her credit for.

"Josephine, Megan Steiner. Megan's firm backs Nicole's lingerie line." He guided his woman to the stool where he'd been sitting and got out three more shot glasses for her from the cabinet. "Megan and Smelly are here to test my smoothies and maybe invest in my idea."

"Maybe?" Megan snorted, pushing a shot glass across the counter. "I'm definitely in, and if Smelly isn't he's a fool. Did you see the business plan, Smells?"

The man nodded as he watched Bull fill the glasses. "It's kind of brilliant. Aggressive marketing plan, too. I like it. I wouldn't expect anything less from a man like Bull Torres."

"This is my basic smoothie." Bull filled their glasses. He should have been watching the reactions from the investors, but his gaze was glued to Josephine Belle's, to see how she liked it.

She blinked in surprise, and then took another delicate sip.

Yes. He grinned and returned his attention to the other two. "You know, Smelly, if we go into business together, we'll be Smelly and Kelly."

The man laughed like it was the funniest thing ever. "One day I'll tell you how I got my nickname. It's a doozy of a story."

Megan rolled her eyes. "Try the other smoothies, Smells."

For the next hour, they discussed branding, distribution, and roll-out strategies. Smelly was a little bit unfocused, but Megan had warned him about that. She'd also told him not to worry, that Smelly kept out of the day-to-day business, only wanting his investment to be paid off in the end.

Bull hadn't been wrong about Megan—she was as sharp as he'd taken her for. He liked her raucous way of talking, too.

Josephine Belle sat there the whole time, listening intently without interfering except to ask for more of one of his juices. His heart swelled when she said she liked it. He was such a sap.

Megan declared that she had places to be and escorted Smelly out of the house with her, leaving Bull and Josephine alone in the kitchen with a lot of dirty shot glasses.

Josephine stood up. "I'll help you clean up."

"No way, babe." He turned her around and trapped her against the counter. He didn't touch her, even though it was killing him. The scent of her tickled his nose and it was all he could do not to bury his nose in her neck. "I've behaved myself long enough. Now you have to come clean about why you're here."

She swallowed audibly, staring at the open

collar of his shirt before her eyes travelled up, over his tattoo, and then to meet his. "Maybe you were right."

"Words I love to hear, but you're going to have to do better than that."

She glared at him. "I was scared, alright? I've been burned in the past, and I guessed if I was attracted to you, you were just as bad as the other guys. You have tattoo on your face, for heaven's sake."

He grinned. "You're attracted to me?"

"*That's* what you're going to take away from all I've said?"

"It's the only thing that came as a surprise to me." He chanced touching her, just a brush of his finger on her hand. But part of him had doubts, so he said, "So you came here and saw my big house, and my business associates, and you thought I wasn't so bad."

She glared at him. "Don't do that. I came here

because I missed your harassment. I'd already de-cided that I wanted you, if you'd have me. I know I behaved badly."

"Actually, you were a total bitch."

"Fine." She rolled her eyes.

"Just calling a spade a spade." He sobered. "You can't deny that you didn't believe I was wor-thy without seeing all this stuff."

"Yes, I can, and I can prove it." She pushed him back and unbuttoned her coat.

He mouth fell open as he saw flashes of red. "You didn't—"

"I did." She pushed the coat off her shoulders and set it on the counter.

He staggered backwards, blown away by the sight of his corset on her body.

It was even better than he'd imagined, and he had a *really* good imagination. It propped her up like she was served especially for him, taunting him with her curves. It hugged her hips, creating a perfect frame for the tiny panties that covered her feminine delights. To top it off, she wore black thigh highs and come-to-me-poppa heels that almost made him swallow his tongue.

How hadn't he noticed? He shook his head.

"Well?" she asked.

He put a hand over his heart. "I think it's stopped."

Her beautiful eyes narrowed, and she sauntered toward him in a way that made him break out in a sweat. "Do you need mouth-to-mouth?"

He managed to nod.

"I can do that." She slid her arms around his neck. "Forever, if you'll let me."

"I'd be crazy not to," he murmured as he pulled her closer.

"I like your kind of crazy," she said, and then she kissed him.

Chapter Twenty-five

JULIE WINCED AS the woman with the comb
yanked her hair for the millionth time. "Are hair-
dressers always so sadistic?"

"I'm a stylist, honey." As if to punish her, the
woman pulled her hair again.

"Ouch." Julie glared at her. The upside to being made up in a private room was that there'd be
no witnesses if she murdered her torturer.

Her second torturer, actually, because the
makeup artist had already visited her. She frowned
at herself in the mirror, trying to find fault with
the woman's work, but, truthfully, she was entranced by the magic the woman had worked on

her. Elise had assured her that she wouldn't look like a clown. She didn't. Her makeup was subtle and barely there, but somehow enhancing.

Hopefully Scott would think so, too.

She reached for the glass of champagne someone had brought her, wincing when her hair pulled and then again when she remembered the glass was long empty. Damn it.

Alexis walked into the room, radiant with joy and happiness. "How are you doing?"

"I'm pretty sure I need to check on the orchids in the main parlor to make sure they're draping properly."

"The flowers look great. Mother told me." Alexis patted her shoulder. "Don't worry. This is going to work out."

"Easy for you to say." Julie pouted. "You're the bride. Shouldn't you be close to puking with nerves? You look way calmer than I feel."

"That's because my fate is signed, sealed, and

delivered. Rob is mine, and I'm already deliriously happy. Today is just a formality." She grinned. "You, on the other hand, don't have anything settled, which is why you're so jittery and unhappy."

"Thanks," Julie said drily, giving the hair lady a dirty look as she twisted her hair tight.

Alexis leaned in. "You're going to be happy, Julie. I'm positive."

She swallowed. There were so many ways Elise's scheme could go wrong, and it wouldn't just be her own life she'd be ruining but Alexis's wedding, too.

Elise breezed in, looking amazing in a flowing pink dress. It looked expensive, but not as expensive as the diamonds dripping around her neck and from her ears.

Julie would have turned around if her hair weren't in a vice grip. "Will there be armed guards at the wedding? To give you a heads up, I may be tempted to commit armed robbery after seeing that necklace."

Elise touched the cascade of glittery jewels. "My mother-in-law gave this to me the day I got married, to welcome me into the family. I've been saving it for Prescott's bride."

Alexis nudged her. "You better start doing my videos so you have the strength to stand up under all that weight."

"Really, Alexis." Elise focused on her daughter, frowning. "Why isn't your hair done yet? The ceremony is in less than an hour."

The stylist sighed, but it was Alexis who said, "Julie needed more primping time than I do."

Julie shot her a glare.

"If you're going to be my sister, you should get used to it now." Alexis winked and then kissed her cheek. "He loves you, Julie," she whispered in her ear. "It's going to work out."

Alexis gave her mother a hug as she floated out of the room.

Elise walked to Julie and wiped her cheek

where Alexis had kissed her. "He does love you. You have nothing to worry about, darling."

She had plenty to worry about. She'd been a bitch to him. He probably decided she was too high maintenance.

But then she remembered the way he looked at her, and the way he always kissed her, and she knew all the doubts were just her fears talking. He loved her, the same way she loved him. She just had to tell him she'd been misguided.

Okay — she'd been an idiot. She started to cover her face with her hand, but then she remembered she had makeup on and caught herself before she ruined an hour's work.

"Julie's hair looks perfect," Elise said to the stylist. "You can focus on Alexis now."

The woman sighed like she was put upon by the world and packed up her station to move to the room where Alexis held court.

"Now, your dress." Elise walked to the wardrobe in the corner of the room and flung the doors open. Inside hung a silver sheath, simple, with a little sparkle to the fabric. A pair of silver strappy shoes sat on the bottom of the cabinet.

Julie reached out to touch the fabric. "It's a fairy princess dress."

"I saw it and knew it was the right one for you. It's not fussy at all, simple and stunning." Elise smiled at it, looking satisfied with herself. Then she faced her. "Which leaves your jewelry."

She glanced at the necklace that could have doubled as a chandelier and shook her head. "That isn't me, Elise."

"Of course it's not. I'd never give this to you. It's not you at all." The woman looked at her like she was insane for even thinking it. She opened a side drawer in the wardrobe and pulled out a small box. She opened it. "This is what I'd give you."

Julie reached out to take the delicate chain.

On the end a teardrop diamond dangled, small and simple.

"It was my mother's. My father gave it to her," Elise said. "It's flawless. The best quality and quite rare, even though it appears unassuming. Like her. Like you."

She ruthlessly suppressed her tears. There was no telling what'd happen if she messed up her makeup. "You're like my fairy godmother."

Elise took her hand and squeezed. "I'd rather be your mother-in-law."

Julie swallowed thickly. "I'll see what I can do about that."

"I have faith in you, and Prescott." Her expression became serious. "I wanted my children to have the happiness I never had. I couldn't have asked for a better woman for my son."

Julie hugged her. "Thank you for everything."

"I did nothing, darling." Elise squeezed her and then stepped back. "Now, I'm going to make sure my daughter is properly taken care of, and I believe you have a man's hand you need to win?"

"Yes." She took the dress from the hanger and, as soon as Elise closed the door behind her, completed the transformation.

She waited until she had the shoes and necklace on to look in the mirror. She gaped at the image, and then made a face just to make sure it was really her.

"I look awesome," she said to her reflection, reaching out to touch it, entranced by the way she shimmered and glowed.

She still saw herself. Elise had been careful not to change her. She may not be wearing jeans, but her hair still had the careless look she was used to, even if it took an hour to achieve. She just looked like a different version of herself.

She liked it, she realized with surprise. Straightening her back, she walked around on the heels, grateful that they were low. When she felt like she had the hang of it, she left the safety of the room and went in search of Scott.

She got to the top of the second floor landing and froze. The foyer downstairs was teeming with people, all elegantly dressed, their jewelry glittering in the dimmed light of the chandeliers and candles.

It was now or never.

Rubbing her hands on her magic dress for courage, she strode down the spiral staircase slowly, despite all the curious gazes on her. She went very slowly. She knew she must look haughty but she was more concerned with tumbling down the stairs in front of all the people than their opinion of her.

Any other time she might have felt like a fish out of water, but she was so worried about how Scott was going to react to seeing her that she couldn't care less about the curious gazes of the San Francisco elite. At the bottom of the steps, she grabbed a glass of champagne from a circulating waiter and downed it before continuing to look him.

She found him to one side of the main parlor, talking to a stunning tall, thin brunette who was dressed in a sleeveless silky black jumpsuit.

Julie forced herself not to care about the woman and focused on Scott instead.

He looked up and met her gaze. Julie wasn't sure how she expected him to react, but she was happy when she saw him light up with hope.

She took a deep breath, feeling hopeful herself, and strode to him. There were a million things she wanted to say, *I'm sorry* highest on her list. What came out of her mouth was "What's your name?"

He looked at her like she'd lost her mind. "You know my name, Julie."

The woman next to him snickered.

Julie shot her a look as Scott said, "Shut up, KT."

"Sorry." The woman didn't look contrite at all. "Um, maybe you guys can move along? This is my hiding spot, and you're calling a lot of attention to it."

Rolling her eyes, Julie grabbed Scott's arm and dragged him to the middle of the room, which was empty. "Just play along, will you? What's your frickin' name, Scott?"

His lips twitched, but he managed to say, "Scott Wright."

She nodded, stepping toward him. "Scott Wright, I'm going to kiss you."

His arms wound around her waist. "Are you a good kisser?"

"You tell me," she whispered as her lips met his.

It was everything it'd been before. It was the stars and moon. It was fairy dust and magic.

It was a promise of the future.

Wrapping her arms around his neck, she

pressed herself to him, liking the way she could feel his warmth through the thin barrier of her dress. As she kissed him, she said, "I think everyone's staring at us."

"They aren't used to a woman mauling a gentleman in his own home." He gripped her waist. "But maybe if we dance, they'll forgive you."

"There's no music playing."

"We don't need music." He looked at her sternly. "But I'm leading."

"Are you going to be this bossy for the rest of our lives together?"

"Are we going to be together for the rest of our lives?" he asked carefully.

"Yes, we are." She glared at him, daring him to say otherwise.

He nodded, sweeping her into an elaborate turn. "I take it you won the competition."

"Actually I forfeited."

"What?" He stopped suddenly, staring at her.

"The competition was the most important thing in your life."

She shook her head. "You were the most important thing in my life. I was just too much of an idiot to realize it. It took your overbearing mother and one crazy actress for me to see how much of an idiot I was."

Scott was still, his gaze boring into hers. Finally, when he spoke, he said, "You really were an idiot."

"I know." She cupped his face. "I hope I can be your idiot forever."

"I'd rather you be my wife," he said, turning his head to kiss her palm.

"Okay." She nodded. "Let's do that, because I love you."

"About time," he said, grinning, as he lifted her up and twirled her around.

Epilogue

One month later...

JULIE STARED AT herself in the full-length mirror. "I look so..."

"Beautiful," Elise said reverently, adjusting the strap of the wedding dress.

"Stunning," Alexis said from where she reclined on the couch drinking champagne.

But it was Sophie's verdict Julie waited for.

Her best friend walked around her, her critical eye taking in every detail of the pewter-colored dress. It was made of a satiny material that clung to her body and flared at the bottom. Sophie had picked it out, saying that the color was great because Julie wouldn't be able to pull off virginal white.

Julie would never admit it, because Sophie would be insufferable after, but she secretly loved the dress. It was comfortable but at the same time made her look like an old-time movie star. Scott loved when she got dressed up, but what made her happy to do it was that when she puttered around in her ratty sweatshirt and shorts, he looked at her like he was the luckiest man in the world.

The only jewelry she wore was the necklace Elise had given her at Alexis's wedding, earrings to match, and the rock Scott had given her when he'd officially proposed.

The ring really did rival Alcatraz. Big and glittering, it sat like a weight on her hand. Scott said he wanted her to remember without a doubt that she was his forever. Like she could forget.

Because Scott wasn't a jewelry type of guy,

she'd gotten him something else to mark him as hers for the rest of his life: a ball and chain. She was going to give it to him tonight, when they kicked off their honeymoon.

Sophie fussed at Julie's hair, rearranging one of the clips, and then she nodded. "You'll do."

Elise gasped in shock.

Before her almost mother-in-law came to her defense, Julie said, "Thanks, Sophie. You look nice, too, even though you've gained a few pounds."

Sophie laughed, the rich, deep laugh the entire world recognized. "You know I love you, right?"

"You know you guys are weird, right?" Alexis said as she stood up. "But that's okay, because the Carrington-Wrights are weird, too."

"We are not," Elise said with a lift of her patrician nose.

"Sure we are, Mom. Have you seen what Scott's wearing today?"

Elise froze. "He wasn't serious about wearing a leopard-print tuxedo?"

"I don't think so, but you never know with him. He's so into animal print," her almost sister said, putting an arm around Elise. Alexis winked at Julie as she guided Elise out of the room. "See you guys down there."

"Really?" Sophie wrinkled her nose when the door closed. "Scott doesn't seem like a leopard-print sort of guy to me."

"He's not. Alexis was giving us time alone." She took a deep breath. "So I'm doing this."

"Yes, and it's going to be awesome, because I planned it all." She rubbed her hands together. "I promised you the wedding of the century, and that's what you're getting."

Julie remembered their bet and shuddered. "Please tell me there aren't going to be any acrobats or people shot out of cannons or anything."

"I promised you the wedding of the decade." Sophie smiled mischievously. She picked up their wedding bouquets, which Julie had insisted on doing herself, and tossed Julie's to her. "Ready to do this?"

"Yes," she said without a doubt. She walked slowly out of the room, careful not to step on her dress. "You know how I know you love me?"

"How?"

"You let me wear wedged flip-flops with my wedding dress."

Sophie nodded. "That's certainly a sign of true love. Or else I didn't want to be embarrassed when you tripped and knocked me down like a bowling pin."

"I see your point."

They reached the main landing and looked down.

There weren't nearly as many people as at

Alexis's wedding. Scott had told Elise he only wanted people who cared about them to attend, and surprisingly his mom had agreed.

Still, there were almost two hundred people, including half of Laurel Heights. And somewhere in the crowd, her parents were hanging out awkwardly.

Whatever. She was glad they came. She wasn't sure they'd step out of their comfort zone long enough to attend.

A chiming bell rang, signalling everyone to the ballroom for the ceremony. She'd wanted to have the wedding outside — the Carrington-Wright mansion had a gorgeous yard — but summer in San Francisco was dicey enough that Elise and Sophie had convinced her she'd be happier indoors.

They waited until everyone had filed into the ballroom to walk downstairs. Sophie walked her, arm in arm, all the way to the ballroom. At the entrance, her best friend turned to her and smiled.

"I feel like I should tell you what to expect on your wedding night, but I suspect you've been doing some experimenting already."

Her cheeks flushed, remembering that morning in the linen closet.

Sophie arched her brow. "You naughty girl. Good for you."

"Shut up."

Sophie grinned and hugged her tight.

Julie hugged her back, feeling so blessed that she had a friend like this.

"Be happy, Julie," Sophie whispered in her ear right before she kissed her cheek. She rubbed off the lipstick that had transferred and then put her million-dollar smile in place. The music changed, and she nodded. "Let's do this, shall we?"

"Yes." Julie took a deep breath as she watched Sophie walk down the aisle. Everyone watched her, because Sophie was fabulous.

And then the music changed again, and she

knew it was her turn. She stood straight, held her flowers in front of her, and walked to her man.

At first, she was blinded by the décor. Sophie had told her she was going to plan the wedding of the century — Julie just hadn't realized it would mean *this*.

It was like a wedding store puked in the ballroom. There were rose petals on the floor, elaborate flower sculptures, bows on the chairs, and streamers hanging from the ceiling. At the end of the room, Scott, KT (who was his best "man"), Sophie, and the officiate waited for her under a gazebo sort of thing that was pretty much a canopy of flowers.

She looked at her fiancé, who shrugged. She could hear what he was thinking loud and clear: *as long as I get to marry you.*

Yes. She walked down the aisle straight to him.

He came out to meet her, taking her hand and drawing her under the umbrella of flowers.

Julie looked up. "This is amazing."

"Your new friend did it," Scott whispered, nodding to the side where Amy from the flower competition looked on with a dreamy expression on her face.

"It's kind of—" Julie searched for the right word.

"Overkill," Scott offered, as the procession music ended.

She snickered.

Grinning, he lifted her chin. "It suits us, because we're both over the top."

"Yes, Prescott, we *do* are." She rolled her eyes.

He kissed her, softly, looking into her eyes the whole time. "I love you, Julie."

"Guys." KT popped her head between them. Her hair was pulled back in a simple knot, emphasizing her sharp cheekbones. "The official dude hasn't said you can do that yet."

"I haven't," the officiate agreed.

"Sorry," Scott said. "My wife is stubborn."

"She's not your wife yet," KT whispered, giving a nervous look at the staring crowd. "I don't know about you, but I'm dying up here in this coat."

Sophie leaned in. "I said you should have worn that tux without the shirt. You'd have looked hot wearing it with only a bow tie around your neck."

KT blushed bright red. "And I said *hell no*. It's bad enough that I'm standing up here." She glared at Scott.

Who looked at Julie with an amused grin. "KT doesn't like being in public."

The officiate cleared his throat. "Maybe we can get on with this? The guests are waiting."

KT tugged at her collar. "Which means you have to try to keep your lips off each other for a few minutes, till the husband-and-wife-forever part."

"We already have forever," Julie said with a smile. And then she kissed her man again, impatient guests be damned.

Also fall in love with Kate Perry's sexy, playful Pillow Talk novels including Playing Doctor and Playing for Keeps...

Playing Doctor

After catching her research partner-slash-fiancé with the intern, Dr. Daphne Donovan returns home to lick her wounds and figure out how to fix her life. It doesn't take a genius to figure it out: being an uber-brilliant Doogie Howser has made her life miserable while all the normal people she knows are happy and content.

There's only one thing to do: become normal. No more being the wunderkind of childhood disease research. All she wants is a regular nine to five job, two-point-five children, a white picket fence, and a blue collar husband.

Except normal isn't all it's cracked up to be,

especially after she meets Ulysses Gray. Gray is everything she doesn't want: smart, incredibly handsome, and a doctor--just like her ex-fiancé. She wants to deny him--and herself--but she can't resist playing doctor...

Playing for Keeps

Since her mother's death more than fifteen years before, Grace Connors has been the matriarch of her family. She has put her own dreams on hold to raise her younger sisters and keep her ex-marine father in line.

So when her sister Nell decides to get married, it's on Grace to put together a wedding that would have made her mother proud. It can't be that hard to organize a party, right?

But then everything falls apart, including her

budding romance with her sexy best friend Pete. Caught in the crossfire with the enemy at her back, will Grace be able to fix it all before she becomes a casualty of love?

Legend of Kate

Kate has tangoed at midnight with a man in blue furry chaps, dueled with flaming swords in the desert, and strutted on bar tops across the world and back. She's been kissed under the Eiffel Tower, had her butt pinched in Florence, and been serenaded in New Orleans. But she found Happy Ever After in San Francisco with her Magic Man.

Kate's the bestselling author of the Laurel Heights Novels, as well as the Family and Love and Guardians of Destiny series. She's been translated into several languages and is quite proud to say she's big in Slovenia. All her books are about strong, independent women who just want love.

Most days, you can find Kate in her favorite café, working on her latest novel. Sometimes she's wearing a tutu. She may or may not have a jeweled dagger strapped to her thigh...

Made in the USA
Lexington, KY
28 January 2014